CHRISTMAS CHEER
A SWEET ROMANTIC COMEDY

NEVER SAY NEVER

REMI CARRINGTON

Copyright ©2020 Pamela Humphrey
All Rights Reserved
Phrey Press
www.phreypress.com
www.remicarrington.com
First Edition

This is a work of fiction. Names, characters, businesses, places, events, and incidents are either the products of the author's imagination or used in a fictitious manner. Any resemblance to actual persons, living or dead, or actual events is purely coincidental.

All rights reserved. This book or any portion thereof may not be reproduced or used in any manner whatsoever without the express written permission of the publisher except for the use of brief quotations in a book review.

❀ Created with Vellum

Christmas Cheer

3 Stories. 3 Happily Ever Afters. Lots of Laughs.

Christmas Love: When Martha mistakes her new boss for the Rent-a-Santa, it leads to a very merry Christmas.

Christmas Sparkle: Bella's most embarrassing moment is how she meets the man of her dreams. But will her family ruin everything?

Christmas Surprise: Josefina's mistakenly sent text leads to Christmas surprise.

CHRISTMAS LOVE

Mistaking her new boss for the Rent-a-Santa makes Christmas memorable.

CHAPTER 1

OWEN

TEN YEARS AGO

Taking over as the new head of a department came with challenges. Besides learning names and personalities, there were office politics to consider. I'd managed people before, but never a whole department.

The company partner who hired me suggested I attend the department Christmas party. I figured that would be a good way to get to see a different side of the employees. And since no one at the party knew who I was, people would be relaxed and more themselves, rather than trying to impress the new boss.

A few minutes early, I walked through the venue until I located the ballroom. I slipped in through the open door in the back and surveyed the room. Holiday music blared from the speakers. An attractive woman walked beside the buffet table, checking a clipboard in her hand as she went. Her light brown hair danced on her shoulders as she moved her head back and forth. "Once Santa gets here, everything will be ready. I can't believe he's late. People will start showing up any time now."

Another woman with short blonde hair handed over a glass of punch. "Martha, relax. Have another glass of punch. It all looks great. People will have fun. They always do."

Martha? In my head, I ran through the list I'd received earlier in the day, which had the names of all the employees in the department. A Martha had been Bob's personal assistant, which meant she was now my personal assistant.

"I'm glad we're having the party earlier this year. Having it the first Saturday of December should give us better attendance." Martha sipped the cranberry-colored beverage. "This is fantastic. So much better than last year."

"That's because I made it." The second woman leaned in closer but didn't lower her voice. "Did you hear the news? They let Bob go."

Martha hugged the clipboard to her chest. "It's so shocking." She didn't seem all that shocked.

"It happened yesterday afternoon. I'm guessing there will be an official announcement on Monday. I heard he was dating someone else in the department. Totally against company policy." Liza flashed a wicked grin. "I have no idea how management found out."

I had a pretty good idea. And now I knew to watch out for Liza. Not that I intended to date anyone within the department or even within the company.

Martha smoothed her red velvet skirt. She was much too young to be Mrs. Claus, but she gave festive a whole new meaning. Thoughts like that would get me fired before I made it to my first full day on the job.

She downed the rest of her punch. "Would you mind getting me another glass?"

"Sure." That devilish grin plastered itself on Liza's face again.

As Martha turned on the tree lights and continued marking items off her list, I popped a soft peppermint in my mouth and slipped out of the room. Once the party got into full swing, I'd make an appearance again, but I wasn't ready to get caught standing in the corner. And Martha or Liza would spot me if I hung around any longer.

When I'd accepted the job, I'd been told all about Bob's violation of company policy. What I hadn't been told was who he'd been dating within the department. That last exchange made me curious about what Liza knew.

Standing near the back entrance of the venue, I crossed my arms, regretting my decision not to wear a coat or jacket. A jacket seemed too formal based on what the partner had said about the party, and I didn't want to keep up with a coat. But the sweater I'd worn wasn't warm enough for standing outside. Walking all the way to my car to get my coat out of the trunk seemed like too much effort.

After only twenty minutes outside, I pulled open the door and slammed right into Martha.

She grabbed my arm and huffed.

Immediately I understood Liza's devilish grin. She'd spiked the punch.

Martha teetered and grabbed onto me with her other hand. "You're late. Where's your suit?"

Late for what?

"I don't have a suit." I hovered my hands near her waist, not wanting to touch her but ready to catch her if gravity pulled her down.

"Lucky for you, I keep a Santa suit in my trunk during this time of year. Just in case." She spun around, then leaned back against me. Quiet for a second, she stayed with her back smashed against my chest.

Her mint-scented shampoo made me crave another peppermint.

I convinced myself that the only reason I remained still, my heart thumping against her back, was because if I moved, she'd fall. And I didn't want that.

"I'm so nervous about impressing our new boss, I think I've made myself sick. Don't tell anyone, but I think he's planning to show up tonight. Arranging everything for this party was my job. And it's important to me that it goes perfectly." She tilted her head and looked up at me. "You're a horrible Santa."

Never before had I cared about how well I could imitate the jolly man in red, but now, I had a strong desire to be a great Santa. "Get me that suit."

She turned to face me. "We need to hurry. Santa is supposed to kick off the party. People are hungry and ready to eat." She grabbed my hand. "Follow me."

I let her drag me out to the parking lot. Clearly, I'd taken leave of my senses.

She opened the trunk of her Volkswagen—I assumed it was hers, but it looked just like mine—and lifted out a big box. "You carry this." After closing the trunk, she fanned herself. "It's a little warm for December. Don't you think?"

"It's in the forties." I was getting the impression Martha didn't imbibe often and that her glasses of punch were catching up to her.

We walked back into the building and I carried the box into the men's room. Martha walked in right behind me.

"We need to get that sweater off you. The collar will show above the red coat, and that would look horrible." She lifted the hem of my sweater.

I grabbed her hands and lowered them to her sides. "How many glasses of punch did you have?"

Her brow furrowed as she reached for my sweater again. "How did you know I had punch?"

"How many?" We played the same game with her hands.

"Four." She fanned herself again. "Why?"

"I think Liza spiked it." I yanked off my sweater without her help.

Martha propped her fists on her hips. "Why would you think that?"

"Because you don't know me, but you followed me into the men's room and tried to take my clothes off."

Tears pooled in her eyes, and she pressed a hand to her mouth. Was she embarrassed or about to be sick? "I have to get out there. She'll get everyone drunk."

"You are going to stay right there." I spun her toward the door. "Once I change, we'll go in there together. But right now, face the door and *do not* turn around."

I dropped my slacks and slid into Santa's red pants. The belt needed extra cinching to guarantee they wouldn't fall down around my ankles during the party. I hadn't even pulled the coat all the way on when I realized my undershirt would be visible. Martha would only try to take it off, so I beat her to it. My undershirt fell to the floor, and I slipped my arms into the red coat.

"There is a back office where I have my purse and coat. We can put your clothes in there." She turned around without asking. "Wow! We should keep that chest covered. It's not that kind of party." She fumbled as she buttoned up my jacket.

When I tried to help, she swatted my hand.

"You're a skinny Santa. You should probably find a different line of work, but right now, you're all I have." Tears slipped down her cheeks.

I had not come prepared for this.

"Please don't cry. I'll be a good Santa." I lifted her chin until her gaze met mine. "I think the party is going to be very merry."

"Say ho, ho, ho. I want to make sure you can at least do that."

I wasn't used to anyone having such little faith in me. After a deep breath, I belted out my best Santa impersonation.

She shrugged. "It'll do." After two steps toward the door, she stopped and grabbed my arm. "I can't go back in there. I'm tipsy. What am I going to do?"

"Stay close to me. And pretend you didn't drink spiked punch." I patted her shoulder. "But whatever you do, don't drink anymore punch. In fact, don't drink anything unless I give it to you. I'm not sure how trustworthy your coworkers are."

"Liza thinks I turned Bob in, but I didn't. She's trying to ruin the party."

I brushed a tear off her cheek. "You can't cry at a Christmas party. Show me your merry face."

Smiling, Martha looped her arm around mine. "I guess I'll be Mrs. Claus for the evening since you said to stay close. And Liza is a bad apple. She's the one with short blonde hair. You didn't hear it from me, and I would never say that to management or the new boss because I wouldn't want to cause trouble for anyone."

"But . . ." I wanted to hear what she never planned to tell the boss.

"She was dating Bob. And I think she wants my job." Martha smiled up at me. "Your eyes are really blue." She trailed a finger along my unshaven cheek. "And you don't even have a beard."

"I'll have to work on that."

Her lips brushed against mine. "Mmm. You taste like peppermint."

It was time to leave the bathroom because I was way too tempted to kiss her back.

"Everyone is waiting on Santa. We should go to the party." I peeked out the door to make sure the hall was empty. "Okay, let's go."

After stashing my clothes, I followed Martha toward the ballroom. Before she opened the door, she shot me a quick panicked glance, then a wide smile spread across her face. "Be merry."

I'd definitely regret playing Santa for the evening, but Martha needed help, and I was the man for the job. All I had to do was entertain the crowd and keep Martha out of trouble. How hard could it be?

She pushed open the door and threw her arms open. "Merry Christmas, everyone! Look who I found." Her arm looped around mine, and she leaned on my arm. "Santa's here."

"Ho, ho, ho!" I patted her hand on my arm and led her around the room, greeting several employees.

Martha warned each of them about the punch.

After a few minutes, she patted my chest, which made me wonder what she was like when she hadn't been drinking. "Now it's time for pictures. I have that corner set up for photos. People always want their picture taken with Santa."

My evening was going from bad to worse.

Before I could suggest we skip pictures, she was dragging me across the room. She eased up next to me and smiled. "Say cheese."

I tucked an arm around her waist and flashed an obligatory smile.

The camera flashed, and my Santa impersonation was now captured on film. I'd probably already been broadcast on social media.

Because I liked the feel of Martha pressed against me a little too much, as soon as she'd gotten her picture, I stepped back.

The double doors opened at the back of the room, and a large, bearded man in a jolly red suit stepped in. "Ho, ho, ho! Merry Christmas!"

Martha teetered on her shiny black heels.

I grabbed her around the waist. "Careful."

"If he's Santa, who are you?" Her green eyes focused on me.

"Owen Reynolds."

Martha passed out in my arms.

CHAPTER 2

MARTHA

I opened my eyes and snapped them closed half a second later. The room was spinning. And worse than that, Owen Reynolds, my new boss, was hovering over me. Even tipsy, I recognized the horror of the situation. "Where am I?"

"We're in the back office."

I lifted my hand and felt around. The velvety stuff next to me didn't feel like upholstery. Reclined, I couldn't figure out where I was. "But I'm lying down." I barely raised my eyelids, peeking out through slits. "And the room is spinning."

"You are only partially lying down. You're in my lap."

I reached out and touched the velvet again. "You're still in the Santa suit?"

Warm fingers brushed my face. "Yes, but I'll change later. I need to take you home. Who can I leave in charge here? I know Liza isn't the answer."

"James." I grabbed a fistful of his red coat and pried my eyes open.

"I'm going to need a description."

"Tall, black gentleman. Has a wonderful smile. And his

wife makes the best chocolate chunk cookies. They have white chocolate chips *and* milk chocolate chunks in them. So yummy." I buried my face in the coat, wishing the world would stay still.

Owen brushed his hand on my hair. "Can he handle Liza?"

"James can handle anyone. No offense, but he should have been Bob's replacement." I slapped a hand over my mouth. Why couldn't I just shut up right now?

It was bad enough I was being cradled by my new boss. Telling him someone else should have gotten the job didn't make that any better. It made it all worse.

I pushed on his chest. "Help me stand up."

"Are you sure?"

"No, but I need to do it anyway." Holding my skirt down, I swung my legs out of his lap. Once I was on my feet, I grabbed the edge of the desk. "Go talk to James, but hurry. I don't feel well at all."

Mr. Reynolds opened the office door. James waited just outside.

"Who are you and why are you in here with her?" Well over six feet tall, James could be intimidating when he decided to be.

My new boss stepped back and put his hands in front of him. "My name is Owen. I think someone spiked the punch or at least the punch they gave to Martha."

"Liza. That's my guess. Is Martha okay?" James pushed past Mr. Reynolds. "How are you?"

"Embarrassed." I blinked, hoping not to cry. "Will you make sure the rest of the night goes okay? I can't stay."

"You got it." James leaned closer. "Do you trust him to take you home?"

I'd asked myself the same question. When I glanced past James, Mr. Reynolds made eye contact. Though I couldn't explain why, I did trust him. The sober parts of my brain screamed that I had good reason to, so I nodded. "That's our new boss. Please don't say anything."

James laughed. "What a way to meet everyone." He turned to face the blue-eyed Santa. "I've never seen Martha drink at parties . . . or ever for that matter. She's a great employee, and you shouldn't hold this—what happened tonight—against her."

I reached around for the chair when the room started moving again.

"I've gathered that. Thank you for your help." Santa stepped closer to me. "James, let me give you my number in case you need anything. But if you could keep this quiet."

"About you being the boss or you taking Martha home?" James had the nerve to look amused.

"Both. I'll introduce myself on Monday at our department meeting." Mr. Reynolds extended his hand. "Thank you again."

"I've got this covered." James waved, then walked back out.

I gathered my purse and coat. "Don't forget the box for the suit. I can't lose that."

"I stuffed my clothes inside. Let's go. Can you walk?"

"Sort of." I gripped his arm. I might not have a job come Monday, but right now I couldn't find it in me to care. Instead, I giggled all the way to the car.

He helped me into the passenger seat.

I grabbed his hand. "How did you get the keys to my car?"

"Your keys are in your hand, and this is my car."

"We match." I could feel my cheeks pulling and knew my grin looked wide and stupid.

"We do, don't we?" He tapped my dress, then pointed at his outfit.

"I was wrong. You're a cute Santa."

He slid in behind the wheel. "Where do you live?"

I rattled off my address, thrilled I could remember.

When the car started moving, I tilted my head back. "Everything is spinning again. I'm going to close my eyes."

All I needed to do now was make it home without getting sick in his car. That was easier said than done.

∽

"Martha!" Mr. Reynolds jostled my shoulder. "Please wake up."

"I didn't get sick, did I?" I wiped drool off my chin.

He sighed. "No, you didn't get sick. Let's get you inside."

"Hang on. Wait. Look." I fumbled with my phone, using my fancy app to turn on my Christmas lights.

My entire yard lit up.

The Christmas carousel went round and round, playing music. Santa waved from atop his sleigh, and lights twinkled all over the front of the house and in the yard.

"Um, wow." My boss scratched at his super sexy stubble. "You like Christmas."

"I *love* Christmas. And I celebrate it twice a year. Now and in July." I leaned closer to him. "Isn't that fun?"

His gaze snapped up to meet mine. Had he been looking at my lips? Why would he do that?

"Mr. Reynolds, thank you for driving me home." I opened my door, put one foot on the ground, then toppled out headfirst. There had to be a better way to get out of the car.

As I tried to get up, strong arms wrapped around me. "You don't drink much, do you?"

"Nope. How can you tell?" I snaked my arms around his neck, clinging to him to stay upright.

"It was just a good guess." He maneuvered us to my front door. "I need your keys."

"They're in my purse."

His face was inches from mine, and I leaned in to taste peppermint again.

He pulled back. "Where is your purse?"

"In the car."

He squeezed his eyes closed and pinched his lips together. "I'm going to sit you down right here. Do. Not. Move."

"Yes, sir, Mr. Reynolds."

"Call me Owen. I'm not sure it will make this any less awkward, but I can hope."

"Okay, Owen."

He hooked my arms around the porch post. "Hold on to this and stay put. I'll be right back."

"Whatever you say, Santa."

CHAPTER 3

OWEN

The inside of her house was as decked out as the outside. And the realization that leaving her alone would be completely irresponsible hit me as I helped her to the sofa.

"When was the last time you ate?" I needed to get her sobered up.

She kicked off her heels. How had she managed to keep them on this long? Then, smiling, she curled up on the sofa. "Yesterday."

"That's crazy. Why haven't you eaten?"

Upright again, she pointed at me. "Did you miss the part where I was planning a party? That takes work. Hard work."

I eased her back down onto the cushions. "I'm going to order a pizza. Where do you keep your coffee?"

"Yuck. I hate coffee." She closed her eyes. "But I like your dimples."

"Don't go to sleep. I want you to eat before you sleep, okay?"

"I don't want pineapple on it."

We had one thing in common.

"Do you have tea? I'll make us some tea."

She nodded, those bright red lips pulled into a wide grin. How much of this would she remember tomorrow?

Lucky for me, I'd remember all of it. But thinking about the feel of her lips on mine was a bad idea right now.

I ordered a large pizza, then wandered into the kitchen.

A bright red kettle with dancing reindeer painted on the side sat next to the stove. I filled it with water and turned on the burner. While the water heated, I dug through cabinets, finding mugs and teabags.

I Googled to see which kind of tea had the most caffeine. She needed all the help she could get.

After a few minutes, I walked back into the living room carrying two mugs of hot tea. The couch was empty. Her little red cape with the white trim lay on the floor next to her black heels. The rest of her dress lay in the hall.

"Martha?"

"Don't come back here."

Thumping and a loud crash made it hard to stay put. "Are you okay?"

"Oops." Giggles echoed down the hall.

That wasn't the answer I was looking for. I set the mugs on the end table. "I'm coming back to check on you."

"Good. You can help me walk back to the couch."

Only one door had light peeking out around it. I knocked. Checking on her involved having my eyes open, but considering what lay in the rest of the house, I thought about closing my eyes as I entered.

Another thump ended my debate.

I shoved open the door and found Martha giggling on the floor. Thankfully, she was wearing pajamas. Red plaid jammies. She couldn't be any cuter if she tried.

"I fell off the bed." She grinned and held her arms out. "Help me."

After looping her arms around my neck, I picked her up and carried her to the couch.

"Thank you." Warm lips pressed to my neck.

Staying here was a dangerous choice.

"Do you have anyone we could call that might stay with you tonight? A boyfriend or a family member?"

Her head swung back and forth. "I don't have a boyfriend." She squinted her eyes and looked at the ceiling. "But I have parents. They are out of town, but I could call my sister."

"Why don't we do that?"

"But you'll have to go pick her up because she's not old enough to drive."

Adding an underage female to the mix was a horrible idea. And I wasn't leaving Martha in the hands of a teenager. "Never mind. Drink your tea. Pizza should be here soon."

Martha picked up the mugs and sipped out of both, alternating between them. It was a good thing I'd made two.

Sitting on the floor beside the sofa, I made a choice that probably made me a bad person. "Tell me about the other people in the office."

She nodded, then shook her head. "But you can't tell anyone. I don't want to get people in trouble."

"Are you always such a nice person?" If someone had spiked my drink, I'd be fighting mad and spilling secrets.

"No one calls me nice." She slid off the sofa and sat next to me on the floor.

My phone rang, and I prayed it wasn't a problem with the pizza. "Hello."

"Mr. Reynolds, things are going well here. I just wanted to let you know that the punch bowl hadn't been spiked. Liza had a special pitcher set aside and was serving Martha out of that one. I'll make sure things get cleaned up when the party is over."

"Maybe Liza can help you with that."

"Oh, I plan on it, Mr. Reynolds. One other thing. Word got around that Santa was the new boss. I didn't breathe a word. I'm not sure who started the rumor. But I'm sending over a picture you might find amusing. Liza misunderstood, so I think your secret is safe for now."

That made me curious. "Please, call me Owen, and I can't thank you enough."

"Is Martha all right?"

She leaned her head on my shoulder.

"She's doing okay. I'm going to make sure she eats. She drank that punch on an empty stomach."

"Thanks for looking out for her. She's a nice lady." James ended the call.

I set the phone on the floor.

"He called me nice." She sighed.

Against my better judgment, I draped an arm around her shoulders. "From what I've seen, you are very nice."

She nestled closer. "James is really good at his job. Derek works hard, but he isn't as productive. Rita is always quiet and great to work with. Liza shows up, but I'm not sure what she does all day. John stays pretty much to himself." Her words trailed off. "Why did you dress up?"

"Because having Santa at the party seemed important to you."

My phone buzzed, and I opened my texts. James had sent a picture of Liza on the other Santa's lap being very friendly.

Martha giggled. "She thought that was you."

The thought horrified me.

But a knock at the door let me avoid responding. "That's probably the pizza."

Martha followed me across the room and hugged me from behind as I paid the driver. She was not making this easy on me.

"Martha, let's go back to the sofa." I clasped her hand.

"Okay." She sat down on the floor.

I wasn't going to be picky about where she sat. "Start eating. Want more tea?"

"Please. But I don't need two mugs."

I managed not to laugh.

When I arrived back in the living room with the tea, three slices had already disappeared.

"Thank you. I was starving." She had a tiny spot of sauce at the corner of her mouth.

Handing her a napkin, I denied myself the pleasure of kissing it off her. The desire alone concerned me. After the time I'd spent with her, I really wanted to know what she was like sober.

She pushed the box toward me. "You can have some too."

With a slice in one hand and my tea in the other, I ate and listened as Martha told me more about life at the office.

After eating three more slices of pizza and downing two more mugs of tea, Martha moved up to the sofa, curled up on her side, and closed her eyes. "Thank you, Owen. I was wrong. You make a great Santa." Snores chased out the last word.

I pulled the red and green blanket off the back of the sofa and draped it over her.

If I left now, I'd worry all night.

CHAPTER 4

MARTHA

With my head pounding, I sat up. Snippets of last night flashed in my head. Had I really tried to take off Owen's clothes? And when had I changed into jammies?

I cradled my head in my hands, hoping he hadn't helped me change. When I spotted my dress lying in the hall, I worried we'd done more than that.

I nudged the man sleeping on my floor. "Hey."

Scrubbing his face, he sat up. "How are you?"

"My head is pounding, and I don't remember much after trying to get your sweater off." I looked at my dress. "I hope I didn't... I mean... we didn't—why are you here?"

He followed my gaze. "I brought you home. We ate pizza. Then you slept. I was afraid to leave you alone. The punch had done a number on you."

"So we didn't..."

"Oh, no! Nothing like that." He stood and stretched. "Now that I know you're okay, I should probably head home."

"I want the Santa suit back."

"Of course, I'll bring it to the office on Monday." He furrowed his brow. "On second thought, let me change now."

I nodded and started making my way down the hall with the help of the wall.

"You don't look okay."

"I can't remember the last time I felt so horrid. Why would people do this on purpose?" I'd watched coworkers get sloshed at parties, but I'd never been drunk. This wasn't any fun.

Owen slipped an arm around my waist. "Lean on my arm. Where are you headed?"

"To the bathroom."

"I'll walk you as far as the door." He flashed a smile and dimples appeared.

Once I'd made it to the bathroom and closed the door, I ridded my body of copious amounts of tea, then took meds for my headache.

Owen was waiting in the hall. "I put the suit back in the box."

"Thanks. Let's turn off the lights. They hurt."

He pulled me to his chest. "I'm so sorry. You should sleep a little more. It's only three in the morning."

"Yeah, but I'm hungry." With my eyes squeezed closed, I relaxed against him.

We definitely couldn't do this at the office.

He stroked my hair. "I'm sorry this happened."

"You probably think I'm a gullible idiot."

He scooped me into his arms. "Nope. What are you hungry for?"

"Pancakes."

"Do you have the ingredients?"

"Yes, I think so. Take me to the kitchen."

He set me in a chair. "Close your eyes. If I need something, I'll ask."

With only light pouring in from the other room, Owen bustled around the kitchen, mixing batter and cooking silver-dollar-sized pancakes. I didn't keep my eyes closed. He was much too good looking for that.

He set a plate in front of me, then placed a platter and the bottle of maple syrup in the center of the table. "I really wish you didn't hate coffee."

"I have a tiny pot under that cabinet. And there is a can of coffee grinds in the freezer. My sister likes to drink coffee. I keep telling her it's not good for her, but she doesn't listen."

"I agree with your sister." He pulled out the mini coffee pot and sighed when the drip started. The man liked his coffee. Cradling his cup as if it were treasure, Owen sat across from me. "Eat up. There's nothing weird about eating pancakes in the middle of the night, right?"

"After tonight, can we just forget all this happened?"

"We can promise not to talk about it." Was that his not-so-subtle way of saying he wouldn't forget?

What else had I done?

I focused on my pancakes.

Owen finished eating and pushed his plate to the side, then wiped his mouth. And when he did, I remembered another snippet.

"I kissed you, didn't I?"

"Yep." He jumped up and poured the last of the coffee into his cup. "But we won't talk about that."

"I am so sorry. I was expecting a nice old man, but you showed up, and I guess the alcohol..."

"The punch made you do it." He chuckled. "We're okay."

"I wouldn't blame you if you fired me." I liked the job, but I wasn't sure how I'd show my face in the office on Monday.

"Are you kidding? It seems to me there are only a few trustworthy people in that office, and you are at the top of the list."

"I hope I didn't say anything horrible about anyone."

He crossed his arms and leaned on the table. "I appreciated what you were willing to tell me."

"If you don't feel like driving, you can sleep on the couch. I'm going to crawl in bed."

"If you don't mind, I think I'll do that." He picked up the plates. "You go sleep. I'll take care of the dishes."

"Thank you." I pushed back from the table.

He stopped in front of me, his hands full of dishes. "You okay?"

"I promise never to do this at the office, but may I hug you?" I hadn't felt so cared for since I had the flu my senior year of high school and my mom made me chicken noodle soup.

The plates clinked as he set them down. "You may."

I buried my face in the curve of his neck, knowing I'd have to force myself not to think of this moment when I was working with him at the office. After hanging on to him way too long, I pulled away. "Make yourself at home."

Shuffling down the hall, I left Owen to clean up my kitchen. Perhaps all of this had been a dream . . . the sort of dream where Santa shows up and has pizza with you and then makes pancakes and cleans up. That made more sense.

I fell into bed, hoping it had all been a dream.

FEELING BETTER than I had in the middle of the night, I walked into the kitchen.

Owen sat at the table, sipping coffee.

Clearly, it hadn't all been a dream.

His dimples showed up, making me want to kiss them.

"Good morning. I wasn't sure how much of last night was my imagination."

"The pancakes were real. And thanks for letting me get more sleep. I needed it. Is your headache better?"

"Mildly."

"I can take you to get your car. And while we're out to get your car, why don't you let me buy you lunch?"

"I want Mexican food." I tried to think of a place where we wouldn't be spotted by anyone from the office. "There is a good place in Dripping Springs."

"Good idea. We'll pick up your car on the way back." He crossed his arms. "We wouldn't want anyone to think that . . ."

"That you are like Bob." I spun around and walked back to my room.

After changing into jeans and a Christmas sweater, I wandered back out to the living room.

He threaded his fingers through his closely cropped hair. "I don't want you to think that—"

"I was joking." I patted his shoulder. "You aren't like Bob."

Bob was handsy and had asked me out more times than I could count. But he'd also asked out every other woman in the building. Liza was the only one who said yes as far as I knew. It wasn't surprising someone had said something to management; it was surprising it had taken so long for it to happen.

Owen opened the front door. "Technically, my start date is Monday."

I whipped around and was eye-level with his chest. Looking up at him, I swallowed. "You aren't my boss?"

"Not until tomorrow." His blue eyes sparkled in the daylight.

It was a good thing I was free all day.

CHAPTER 5

OWEN

I slid into the booth, well aware that asking Martha to lunch was the worst thing I could do for my career. Starting tomorrow morning, I'd be working with her.

She peeked at me over the top of the menu. "How long have you lived in Austin?" The menu moved back up, blocking her face.

"Three years."

She grinned as she poked her head around the side. "Where are you from?"

"Houston." I broke a tortilla chip in half and dipped one piece in salsa. "What about you?"

"I've lived in Austin all my life."

"Have you always loved Christmas?" I could've guessed the answer, but watching her green eyes twinkle made it worth asking.

"Always. And then when I was in high school, I learned about Christmas in July, and I fell in love even more." She set her menu aside and leaned forward. "When I was in college, my drinking friends used to go out for Mexican food the next morning, so I thought I'd try it."

Why did she have to be so adorable?

"I've heard menudo is supposed to be good for that."

She opened the menu, and her eyes widened. "I'm not sure I'd like that."

"It's good, but it's not for everyone."

"I'm sticking with enchiladas."

"Always a good choice." I ate another chip, reminding myself that this wasn't a date. We were just two people having lunch. Together. Far away from where we lived so that no one would see us.

Martha smiled. "You got quite the introduction to our department. And I totally understand that this is not a date. But after what happened, this makes it less awkward for me. If you'd left me at my house and I hadn't seen you until Monday, I would've been a complete mess."

"We wouldn't want that." Now I felt justified in asking her. And if lunch made her more comfortable, all day would be even better, right? "Maybe after lunch we should drive through the Hill Country."

"Fun! There are cute Christmas shops in some of those little towns. Have you ever been to Johnson City at night during the holiday season?"

I shook my head, eager to hear the reason for her excitement.

"They drape the courthouse in lights. And the electric cooperative there fills the trees with thousands and thousands of lights."

"We should go. It's almost one now. We can find stuff to do for a few hours, right?"

"You don't even have a coat."

"It's in my trunk." I couldn't think of a good reason not to spend the entire day with her, other than—you know—my job.

After a little while, the waitress set food on the table.

Conversation continued between bites as Martha and I devoured our food. We swapped stories about high school, then college. And she told me about her favorite Christmas. I couldn't have asked for better company.

Mixing her refried beans into her rice, she glanced up. "I feel like I should warn you that Liza will repeatedly try to come onto you. She likes—um, how should I say this—special treatment."

"I figured that out from the picture James sent me. She'll be pretty disappointed when I show up instead of the old guy."

"And she'll hate me because I was hanging all over you and then left the party with you." Martha closed her eyes and shook her head. "I truly embarrassed myself."

"You could probably file charges on Liza. What she did was wrong."

She shrugged. "I don't know how I'd prove it."

"I think she admitted it to James."

"That would put him in a horrible situation at work. I don't want to do that to him. He doesn't need more stress. He'll be upset—never mind."

I'd known the woman less than twenty-four hours, and I could tell what she didn't want to say. "He'll be upset that someone from the outside was hired to lead the department."

"I didn't want you to feel bad. It's not your fault. I just feel horrible for James. He's been in that number two spot for years." She waved her fork in the air as she talked. "But you seem like a genuinely nice guy."

"Do I?"

She glanced up. "I have mixed feelings about working for you."

"You think I'll be a bad boss?" I could pretend I didn't know what she really meant.

Head shaking back and forth, she went back to stirring her beans into her rice. "This might've been a bad idea."

"You don't like the enchiladas?"

She shoved her plate to the side. "Please don't let Liza get you fired."

"I don't plan to get fired." But I also hadn't planned to invite my soon-to-be personal assistant to lunch . . . or stay the night at her house or make her pancakes in the middle of the night.

I needed to decide on some boundaries. The one thing I most wanted to do—kiss her—would only complicate things come tomorrow morning. We were two friends at lunch. How did friends behave?

She sipped her sweet tea. "Thanks for lunch."

"You're welcome. Where should we head first?"

Turning her phone so that I could see the screen, she pointed. "These are the Christmas stores in the area."

"We'll work our way down the list."

WEARING A BEAUTIFUL SMILE, Martha spun in a circle under the holiday lights, her arms spread wide. "I should stop before I fall over."

I shoved my hands in the pockets of my coat. "You look very merry."

"And you look like a Grinch. Why aren't you smiling?"

Possibly because I'd just met someone I wanted to see again but couldn't unless I gave up my job. Walking away from a great career opportunity after spending one day with someone felt foolish.

"Sorry." I flashed a toothy smile. "This better?"

She looped her arm around mine. "Let's go get a picture with Santa. He looks the part."

"That was poorly veiled."

"We'll do well working together. You understand me. It wasn't meant to be veiled at all." She rubbed my arm. "Communication is important in the workplace."

We waited until the family ahead of us convinced their little kids to smile.

Then Martha dropped onto the bench beside Santa and patted the space next to her. I sat down and leaned close. For her, I had no trouble smiling.

The helper elf snapped a photo, then Martha jumped up to order a copy.

Mr. Claus leaned toward me. "What do you want for Christmas?"

"Something I can't have." Today had been the best day in a long time and the biggest mistake I'd made . . . probably ever.

He tapped the side of his nose. It was good that the man in red would keep my secret.

I shook his hand before meeting up with Martha. "How did it turn out?"

"It's great. And don't worry. I won't pin it up at my desk. But I want to remember today. Always." She smiled up at me but didn't bump shoulders with me like she'd done earlier.

Stuffing my hands back into my pockets, I nodded. "It's been a good day."

"I'm trying to decide what you need to know before you start work tomorrow. Oh! On Fridays in December, most of us dress festively."

"Do you wear your pretty red Christmas dress every Friday?" I liked that dress.

She rolled her eyes. "Of course not. I have a different dress for every week. I think this Friday, I'm going to wear my elf getup. I also have a dress that has sugar plum fairies on it. It's really a pretty dress."

"Do you decorate your house in July?"

"You better believe it. But I only give small gifts to my family. Nothing huge." She stopped as we reached the edge of the light display and looked back toward Santa.

"And Santa?"

"I have a Christmas in July party every year and arrange for Santa to show up. Maybe if you aren't busy, you can moonlight as Santa one more time."

"Maybe so." I didn't need to think about donning her Santa suit and having her smiling beside me. But last night was like a news reel in my head playing on repeat. I nodded toward a food truck. "Hot chocolate?"

"No thanks. I'm stuffed from dinner. My steak was amazing." She crossed her arms.

The shift in the evening was unmistakable. This wasn't just the end of our day together. It was the end of what could have been an exciting beginning.

I shivered and pulled my coat tighter when the wind gusted. "The temps are dropping."

She rubbed her mittens together. "We should probably head back so I can get my car. It's getting late, and we both have to be at work in the morning."

"Let's head back to the car."

Instead of walking right beside me, she kept her distance. Her arms stayed crossed, and mine remained in my pockets until I opened the door for her.

"I had fun today." I held out my hand to help her in.

She clasped it and held on even after she was in her seat. "I did too. But tomorrow is another day."

The reminder felt like a punch in the gut. "Yep."

I wasn't looking forward to Monday.

CHAPTER 6

MARTHA

I applied my lipstick, giving myself a pep talk. "He's your boss. Owen is nothing more than that."

Picking up the red Santa coat off my bed, I gave it a sniff. Why did he have to be my boss?

I wasn't about to quit my job because of one perfect day. Shaking my head, I tried to imagine explaining that to my father.

Leftover pancakes provided a quick breakfast, which made it easy to get to the office early. I wanted to have coffee ready and waiting when Owen showed up at work.

The office was only ten minutes away if I hit traffic just right. Today I left early enough that it only took me nine minutes to get to work. So far, my Monday was off to a good start.

The parking lot was still mostly empty, and as I hurried toward the elevators, the doors started to close. I stuck my hand in just in time, and the doors opened.

Owen smiled. "Good morning." He held out a tall cup. "I stopped for coffee and got you a tea."

Good looking and nice? It wasn't fair.

"Thanks. I came in early to get coffee ready. I didn't expect you in yet." The chai tea was sweetened just right.

"I have to spend some time with HR first thing, then I'll be in my office. What time is the department meeting?"

"Ten. I scheduled it late Friday, so some people won't see the meeting alert until they arrive this morning." The doors opened, and I stepped out onto the seventh floor. "Have you seen your office?"

"Briefly during my super-secret interview a few weekends ago."

"Come on. I'll give you a quick tour if you have a few minutes. You can at least hang your coat in your office. Surely, you don't want to carry it around with you all day."

"I don't." He hurried past me to open the door to our office suite. "Do you always come into the office this early?"

"Usually. If I'm here before everyone else, I'm more productive." I stopped and faced him. "I didn't mean for that to sound like you are impeding my productivity or anything like that."

"I'm glad to hear that because I like to be in early, and I wouldn't want to interfere with your routine."

"You're the boss. I can adapt." I needed that reminder.

After setting my tea and coat at my desk, I turned on the Christmas tree lights before leading him into the office right next to mine. A wall of windows with a door in the middle connected both offices, but the blinds were always pulled closed. Not once while I'd worked that job had the door been opened.

Compared to my office, his was much bigger and had a better view.

"This is it. There is a coat rack in the corner and a few hangers in the closet if you need to keep a change of clothes at the office. The kitchenette is stocked with a few snacks—I'll make sure to order some peppermints—and I usually make coffee every morning. Let me know what snacks you like, and I'll make sure those are ordered. If you like a certain type of pen, let me know, and I'll get them." I glanced at the cup in his hand. "Would you like me to make a fresh pot of coffee?"

He lifted his cup. "This'll be enough for me right now. Maybe after I come back from HR."

"Just let me know." I deserved an award. After being around him alone for fifteen minutes, I'd kept it all strictly professional. This wouldn't be so hard. "If you need anything, I'm right next door."

Settled at my desk, I sipped my tea and worked down my to-do list, trying not to think about how Owen looked with that Santa coat hanging open and his bare chest showing. Those thoughts were not professional.

Fifteen minutes later, he poked his head in the door. "I'm off to sign papers and whatnot."

"To become an official employee?" I wanted to kick myself as soon as I said it.

He bit his bottom lip. "Right. If you need me, you can message me."

"I don't have your number."

"Oh, let me give it to you." He crossed the room and scratched out his number on the notepad I pushed toward him. "When I get back, I should probably get yours . . . just in case."

"I'll text you my number." I folded my hands in my lap where they couldn't accidentally touch him. "Text me when you're on your way back, and I'll start coffee."

"Great." He double tapped my desk. "I'll see you in a bit."

In his nicely fitted suit and shiny wingtips, he looked amazing. I just wasn't supposed to notice. How would I survive the chatter in the breakroom after he was introduced as the boss?

Working, I stayed in my office when the other employees arrived, but I listened. Liza's desk was just outside my office, and that was the hub of gossip.

Liza tucked her purse in her drawer and then freshened her lipstick with a little compact mirror. "Rita, is he here yet? I think I scored a few good points on Saturday night."

Rita stepped out of her office and crossed her arms. "I haven't seen him, but the office light is on, so he's around. That's probably what the meeting is about."

"Meeting?" Liza picked up her coffee mug.

"Check your calendar." Rita waved at me, then slipped back into her office. In her forties, she carried herself with confidence and had perfected her tone to be able to put people in their place with only a few words.

Was it possible that Liza wasn't going to intrude and prod for information about how her stunt turned out at the party?

Any hope she'd start working was dashed when she appeared in my doorway. "What happened on Saturday? You left so suddenly. Were you sick?"

"After not eating all day, it was too much. I went home early."

"Your date was cute. And it was sweet that y'all showed up in matching outfits."

"He's very nice, but he wasn't my date." I could feel a headache coming on.

She dropped into a chair. "Oh? I just figured since he left at the same time you did that you left together."

"How was the rest of the party?"

"Great fun!" She leaned forward, flashing a conspiratorial smile. "I heard that our new boss, Bob's replacement, showed up at the party dressed as Santa. So I made nice. Always want to be on the boss's good side."

"Of course." I continued working, hoping that she'd take a hint and walk away.

"Have you met him?" Liza pointed toward Owen's office.

I picked up my cup of tea, glad that it was still warm. "Yes."

"Come on. Say more than that." She sipped her coffee. "I hope you didn't get in any trouble because you left the party early."

"No. It was fine." It had caused me trouble, but not anything I would discuss with Liza.

My trouble was wishing I could date my boss. But the company policy left no gray areas. I still didn't understand why Liza was still with the company. In the past, both offenders were let go. That was what I kept reminding myself. It was more than my job on the line. It was Owen's. I'd never put his job in jeopardy.

And I had a reputation to uphold since my father was one of the partners. Breaking company policy would make him look bad. Another reason to keep my feelings corralled.

Fifteen minutes before the meeting was supposed to start, I set up the conference room with coffee and breakfast pastries, which had been delivered that morning. Once everything was set, I knocked as I slipped into Owen's office to brew him a fresh pot of coffee.

"Hey."

I froze. "I'm so sorry to barge in. I didn't think you were in here." I pointed at the small kitchenette in the corner. "I was going to brew a pot of coffee. I have coffee and pastries set up in the conference room."

He crossed the room and closed the door the rest of the way. "Whatever you have in the conference room is fine for now. Has anyone given you trouble about the party?"

"No, sir."

"This isn't going to work if you call me sir." He rested a hip on the edge of his desk.

"Okay, *Owen*. Liza mentioned me leaving the party early,

but I told her I didn't feel well and went home. I don't even think she knows for sure that we left together. But I'm sure she suspects it."

"Well, if she brings it up at the meeting, let me handle it." He crossed his arms. "If you don't mind."

"Sure." I checked the time. "It's time for the meeting. We should—or rather I should go to the conference room."

"I'll walk with you. Talking to my administrative assistant isn't weird, is it?" He nudged my shoulder before opening the door.

"No. Not weird at all." Wanting to hug him, that was weird.

CHAPTER 7

OWEN

I pulled open the conference room door and let Martha enter first. She dropped into a seat, and I sat down next to her.

Whispers surrounded the table, then silenced when Mr. Morgan, one of the partners entered the room. "Good morning. Thank you for meeting on short notice." He nodded at Martha.

Had he told her about Bob? Martha seemed to know before Liza broke the news.

Mr. Morgan folded his arms. "Friday was Bob Smith's last day here at Morgan and Steiner. We wish him the best in his new endeavors. I'd like to introduce you to the new head of the department, Owen Reynolds." He pointed at me.

I heard a chair topple as I stepped to the front. When I turned around, Liza glared at me from the floor. Was it my fault she'd flirted with the wrong Santa?

I smiled.

She pushed up off the floor and righted her chair. In front of Mr. Morgan, Liza had much less to say. I'd have to remember that.

I made a point not to cross my arms so I wouldn't appear defensive or closed off. "Good morning. Some of you might recognize me from the party on Friday. It was fun to meet so many of you. I am sorry that I had to leave in a hurry that night. I look forward to working with all of you."

Mr. Morgan patted me on the back. "We are excited about having Owen here. He'll be great. Are there any questions before I go?" He glanced at a very expensive watch.

Liza cleared her throat. "Why was Bob let go?"

Mr. Morgan rested his hands on the table and scanned the faces around the table before answering. "At Morgan and Steiner, we take company policy seriously. Mr. Smith violated that policy."

I swallowed, wishing I'd poured myself a cup of coffee. Mr. Morgan probably would not approve of my outing with Martha yesterday. In hindsight, my decision seemed like it was based on a technicality.

"Any other questions?" Mr. Morgan glanced at Martha.

She shook her head.

"All right then. I'm going to go. Thank you for your time. Owen, do you have anything else to add?"

"Just that my door is open today. I'd love to have a few minutes with each of you." I glanced at Martha, and she gave a slight nod. "Martha will coordinate times. Until I learn the system, she's in charge of my schedule."

Polite laughter followed my poor attempt at humor.

Martha didn't wait for me to leave the room. She slipped out right after Mr. Morgan.

After shaking hands with people, I hurried back to my office.

Mr. Morgan waited in one of the high back chairs. "I think that went well."

"I do too." Movement caught my attention, and I noticed

Martha making coffee. "It went more smoothly than I anticipated."

He stood. "If you need anything, Martha can help you. She's the best."

"Thank you, Mr. Morgan."

He waggled his finger at me. "Paul."

I nodded.

After a quick wink in Martha's direction, he strolled out of the room. For a company so strict about company policy, his lack of formality struck me as odd.

"I'm almost done with the coffee, then I'll leave you alone."

I swung my office door closed. "About yesterday..."

She shook her head. "I'd prefer that we avoid that topic." Leaning down, she pulled napkins out of a lower cabinet.

"Why are these blinds closed? Is that a door in the middle of the wall?" I flipped switches and pushed buttons on the wall panel, hoping to find the one that opened the blinds. After a few tries, I found the right one.

Martha slowly turned around. "There is a door. Bob never used it. He preferred the blinds drawn at all times."

"I like them open. You don't mind, do you?"

"Not at all." It wasn't the first time she'd said that phrase, and it seemed like maybe she meant the opposite.

"If you do mind, I can close them."

The same smile from yesterday, a very genuine and alluring one, spread across her face. "I don't mind."

I stood close enough so that I could keep my voice low, but far enough away that if anyone walked into her office and saw us through the wall of windows, there would be no gossip. "I'd especially appreciate it when I have certain employees in the office."

She stepped closer. "You are absolutely nothing like Bob."

Before I could respond, Liza stepped into Martha's office.

"People are already lining up to get on the schedule it seems."

"Might as well tackle the toughest ones first." Martha handed me a cup of coffee. "Black. That is how you like it, right?"

"Yes, thank you." I moved behind my desk and took a seat.

Martha might be the best part of the job and the worst. Mr. Morgan called her the best, and so far, I couldn't disagree. Not dating her because of company policy—that was the worst.

She walked into her office. Her desk was situated so that I was treated to a view of her face. From a work standpoint, it would make catching her eye and getting her attention much easier. From a personal standpoint—I didn't need to think about that.

Martha glanced up and asked her question with a subtle lift of her eyebrows.

I motioned for her to send Liza in.

As Liza sashayed into my office, I gathered my wits. "Have a seat."

She perched on the edge of my desk. "I did not expect *you*."

I stood and pointed at the chairs. "In a chair, please."

"Sure." She moved to a chair. "I'm so glad you're here. It was time for a change in the department. And whatever you need, I am willing to help." She leaned forward. "*Whatever* you need."

"I appreciate that. With everyone doing their job, this department will be productive. I have no doubt about that."

"Right. Well, I should do that . . . my job." Liza glanced over her shoulder before walking out.

I closed my office door, then opened the door leading to Martha's office. "One down."

"Let me show you the calendar app." She walked around her desk and brushed past me, leaving a lingering scent of what I imagined sugarplums smelled like.

The woman did love all things Christmas.

CHAPTER 8

MARTHA

I ducked into the break room to make myself a cup of hot tea. I'd avoided it most of the day, but I really wanted a cup of tea. Thankfully, when I walked in, the room was empty.

That lasted about thirty seconds. Liza strolled in with Kelly, a fairly new member of our team.

"Martha! Just who I was hoping to see. Want to switch jobs? Because I would *love* to work with that man. He's so . . . mmm." Liza filled her coffee mug. "Don't you think?"

"He seems like he'll do very well as the new department head." I couldn't have sounded more stupid if I tried.

"Martha, no one in management is listening to us. Be yourself." Liza hated when I didn't join in with her chatter.

I shot a glance at Kelly. "I'm not sure Owen would appreciate me talking about him in the break room."

Kelly giggled. "First name basis. That was quick." She was spending way too much time around Liza.

I poured hot water into my mug and bounced the tea bag up and down. "I need to get back to work."

"Back to *Owen*?" Liza laughed.

It wouldn't be easy working with him. Just hearing Liza and Kelly talk about him had my jealousy flaring. What was I going to do?

∽

I DROPPED my purse near the door and kicked off my shoes as soon as I walked into my bedroom. The day had gone better than I'd expected, but my attraction to Owen hadn't waned.

The expected phone call came just after I'd pulled on my leggings and shirt. "Hi, Dad."

"Hey there, darling." Dad rarely called to discuss work, but there were occasions when he did. This one didn't surprise me.

I wandered out to the kitchen with the phone tucked between my ear and shoulder. "I'm guessing you want to know how the new hire is doing."

"You know me well. I interviewed him personally, so I'm hoping he does a good job."

Telling my dad that he should have hired James would not change the situation. He was like a cat; something had to be his idea before he'd follow through with it. I also didn't want to give him any hint that Owen hadn't had a good first day.

"Owen Reynolds is polite and smart. I think he'll be a great asset to the department."

Owen also smelled amazing and made tasty pancakes. But I wasn't about to mention either of those facts to my father.

"I'm glad to hear that. When I heard about Mr. Smith's behavior, I was angry that you had to put up with that. That's why I interviewed Owen myself."

"He's nothing like Bob, Dad."

"That's a relief. Well, I won't keep you. If you have any trouble though . . ."

"I know. Does Mom need me to come set up for the

party on Saturday?" Helping with the holiday party my parents hosted for the department heads was on my calendar every year. It was an opportunity to decorate my little heart out.

He chuckled. "Always. I hope this year you won't stay in the other room. You're my daughter, and therefore, invited to my party."

"I'll think about it."

"It's not like the department heads don't know that you're my daughter. Will we see you for dinner on Friday?"

"I'll be there."

"Love you." He ended the call.

All the department heads except one.

Dad and I didn't make a secret of our family connection, but I didn't bring it up unless asked. When people discovered the relationship, the way they treated me changed. What would happen when Owen discovered that I was the daughter of Paul Morgan, founding partner of Morgan and Steiner?

Flustered at the thought, I picked up the Santa coat off my bed. It still smelled of Owen's cologne. I'd wait to get it cleaned, but sleeping with it at night wouldn't make days at the office easier. After folding the pants and the coat into the box, I glanced around for the hat. I searched high and low but didn't find it.

Driven by the need to have the entire costume, I texted Owen: *Do you have my Santa hat?*

He replied right away. *I'll look in my car.*

While I waited for a follow-up response, I started dinner. The recipes for one-pot pasta dinners had made healthy eating so much easier.

Only a few minutes later, he replied again. *Sorry, yes. It's in the backseat of my car. I'll drop it by your place in a bit if that's okay.*

Sounds good. Thanks. I was much too excited about Owen coming back to my house.

Ten minutes later, I opened the door when he rang the bell. "Hi." It was awkward seeing him again after we spent all day being professional in the office. Then to make things even more awkward, my timer beeped. "Come in for a sec. I have to get my dinner off the stove."

He followed me into the kitchen. "Smells good."

"There's plenty if you'd like some." I dumped the pasta into a large bowl.

Owen pursed his lips, and the conversation in his head might as well have been written on his forehead. "Sure. It looks amazing." He loosened his tie, then slipped it off.

I refrained from fanning myself.

"I set the Santa hat on your sofa." He walked up beside me. "I can carry that for you."

"Just put it in the center of the table. I'll grab bowls and silverware."

"Christmas dishes. Why doesn't that surprise me? Do you have a separate set for summer?"

"I like having festive dinnerware. And I don't have a separate summer set." I poked at my pasta, feeling a bit defensive.

"I wasn't making fun of your choices, Martha." He bumped my foot. "I find your love of Christmas rather endearing."

"Most people think it's too much, so I'm usually on the defense."

"I don't think it's too much." Why did he have to make it harder to keep my feelings reined in?

"You're sweet. Eat up." I nudged the serving bowl toward him.

He mounded lots of pasta into his bowl. "This looks so much better than the frozen dinner I was going to have at home."

During dinner, we talked about the day. Owen asked questions about office politics, and I answered carefully.

When we'd finished eating, I picked up the bowls and set them in the sink. "I have brownies and ice cream if you'd like dessert. I usually top it with peppermint crumbles."

"Peppermint? Yes."

We moved to the couch, and for the next three hours, we talked. Work wasn't mentioned once.

I needed to look up the definition of dating. It probably involved romantic gestures like kissing, and we were doing none of that. Surely there wasn't a company policy against enjoying someone's company.

CHAPTER 9

OWEN

Tuesday morning, I stopped at the coffee shop and glanced over the selection of teas, trying to remember what varieties Martha had in her cabinet.

I ordered her an English breakfast tea, and I got a tall drip coffee for myself.

Dinner at her house had been unexpected and wonderful. Not only was she a good cook, I loved being around her.

While I couldn't justify having dinner with her every night, I might be able to swing a lunch with her once or twice a week. If I invited others from the department, it definitely wouldn't be a date.

Halfway to the office, my phone rang. "Hey, Lia, what's up?"

"How's the new job?"

"So far, so good."

Ophelia enjoyed being a little sister. "Do you have a cute secretary who sits on the edge of your desk to take memos?"

"Did you suffer a head trauma? You're aware of what decade this is, aren't you?"

Bubbling laughter came through the line. "You're so fun to tease. I'm headed to class. I'll talk to you later. Maybe you can buy me dinner."

"Sure. Text me. Dinner sounds good." As the big brother, I made sure she enjoyed a nice dinner out every so often.

As the little sister, she called to tease me just for fun.

I made it to the office before Martha. It wasn't a competition. The only important thing to me was getting to see her for a few minutes before others made it into the office.

I set the tea on her desk and waited.

Seven minutes later, Martha stepped into her office and smiled when her gaze landed on the cup of tea. Why was I trying to score points with someone who I was not going to ask out?

She picked up the cup and walked into my office. "Do you sleep at all?"

I watched as she sipped her tea. My aim was to figure out her favorite and make that part of her mornings.

"English Breakfast. Are you rotating through all the types of tea they have?"

I stood, which put her eye-level with my chest. "Until I figure out your favorite." That sounded way too much like flirting.

She bit her bottom lip, then held out my tie. "You left this."

"I hadn't even noticed."

"Not dating would be simpler if items of clothing weren't being exchanged somehow." She looked up at me, her lashes shrouding those green eyes.

I reached for the tie, wrapping my hand around hers. "I could joke that I'd intentionally left it so I could get another free dinner." What was I doing? I yanked my hand back. "But I didn't. My mind was just on other things."

"Well, I'll let you work. When you want me—"

I wanted her. I wanted to sit next to her and hear her laugh. I wanted to feel her soft lips dancing against mine. And I wanted to hold her while she talked about all things Christmas and those green eyes twinkled. "I'm sure they have a good reason for the company policy, but I don't like it." I'd said too much and moved away before I followed through on my thoughts. "That said, I'll try to be better at following policy. I'm sorry if I've made you uncomfortable."

"You haven't." She grazed her fingers on my wrist. "Let me know when you want fresh coffee."

Somehow, I managed to get work done with Martha just on the other side of the glass wall. When it was close to lunchtime, I walked into her office. "Hi. Do you have lunch plans?"

Her eyes widened, and she gave a subtle shake of her head. "We probably shouldn't . . ."

There was wisdom in those words, but what was wrong with having lunch with several people?

"I thought about taking the department to lunch. My treat."

She moved around the desk and clasped my arm. "Owen, there are twelve people in the department. You're going to take all of them to lunch?"

"Sure. I'd appreciate if you stay close in case I have trouble with names." I flashed her a smile.

"All right, but only because you showed off the dimples." Now, she was the one flirting. "Should I let everyone know?"

I nodded. "Thanks. We'll meet outside your office in fifteen minutes. And you can choose the restaurant."

It might cost me a large sum, but I'd get to have lunch with Martha. She was my friend. I wanted to get to know her better. But I didn't want anyone to get the wrong idea because we were definitely not dating.

CHAPTER 10

MARTHA

*L*unch had been interesting. Talking to him was as easy as falling out of bed. I'd done that a time or two. His dimples made me want to kiss him, and his blue eyes made me want to melt.

After lunch, I focused on my tasks. Working with the blinds open made for an interesting dynamic. Occasionally, when I glanced up, Owen looked away as if he'd been caught watching me. Other times, he didn't look away. He only smiled.

But late in the afternoon, when I heard my dad walk into Owen's office, I kept my eyes on my computer screen. I didn't want my dad catching any hint of the chemistry happening between me and Owen.

"Hello, Owen." My dad's booming voice commanded attention.

The door between our offices had been propped open since Monday morning, so I could hear every word my dad uttered.

I couldn't resist a peek.

Dad dropped into a chair. "How have the first two days been?"

Owen showed no hint of nervousness. Relaxed and confidant, he was more than attractive. "Good. Things are going well."

"Very good. I sent you the last quarter reports and the projections for next quarter. I know you are probably still reading through everything I gave you yesterday."

Owen patted a stack of papers. "I'm working my way through it."

Dad laughed. "If you have questions and I'm not around, Martha or James can help you. I just stopped by to see how things were going and to remind you about the party on Saturday."

"Yes. I have it in my calendar."

"Great. Mrs. Morgan is looking forward to meeting you. Martha has all the information." Dad stood and walked to the door. "Make sure you bring a date."

I counted to ten before looking up. Owen met my gaze, and the apology etched in his brow made it hard to smile.

Perhaps I'd skip the Christmas party this year.

WEDNESDAY MORNING, I was in the office before a cup of tea had appeared on my desk. After turning on Christmas lights, I walked into Owen's office and pulled out what I needed to make coffee. So far, he'd shown up every morning with his own cup, so I waited a bit to make coffee, but if today was different, I wanted to be ready.

"Good morning." Owen walked straight to the kitchenette and leaned against the counter. "Here's a cup of Earl Grey."

"Thank you."

"I still don't know your favorite. I know what teachers

you hated in middle school, how many times you snuck out your bedroom window, and the names of all the pets you had growing up, but I don't know what your favorite tea is." He sipped his coffee, eyeing me over the rim of the cup.

"Chai."

"Good to know. Yesterday was fun. It was nice getting to know people over lunch." He'd spent most of his time talking to me. "Is the conference room available during lunch today? I thought maybe we'd order in and see who wants to join us."

"I can check the calendar."

He moved away and let out a breath slowly.

"Anything I can help you with?" It wasn't hard to read his stress level.

He leaned on his desk. "After taking my sister to dinner last night, I spent hours going through reports and projections and other stuff. I'm getting buried in the details."

"I'll block out an hour this morning, and I can give you an overview. Once you have the big picture, everything else will make sense."

"Why aren't you doing my job?"

That was easy to answer. "I don't want your job. I like mine just fine."

He smiled, and my heart fluttered. "Thanks for carving out time to help me."

"I could say the same." I'd never forget what he did for me the night of the party. And frustratingly, I couldn't forget kissing him. I really wanted him to kiss me back.

During lunch in the conference room, I thought about that a lot.

CHAPTER 11

OWEN

Thursday afternoon, I sat at my desk, and my brain felt like it was on a hamster wheel. Who could I take to the Christmas party? Trying to think of someone to ask was made harder by the image of Martha in her little Christmas dress.

After closing the door that joined my office to Martha's, I called my sister. "Lia, I need a plus one for a Christmas party on Saturday. Have any friends that would go with me on short notice?"

She laughed. "I have about twenty friends who would think Christmas came early if they got to go out with you."

"I just want a date for the evening. No romance. No expectations. No second date."

"I'll call around. You'll hear back from me within the hour. Blonde or brunette?"

I glanced up as Martha leaned over, her golden locks hanging down and catching the light from the window. Now, her hair looked blonde.

"I don't care. Surprise me."

"Owen, seriously? You have no preference?" Lia sounded confused.

"Ophelia, if I planned to start a relationship with someone, I might care, but I just need someone who will go and not embarrass me in front of the partners. One party. That's it."

"You made your point. I'll call you soon." She ended the call but followed with a text: *You planning to stay single forever?*

I had no interest in discussing my love life or lack thereof with my sister, but using her to find a date made that topic harder to avoid. I didn't bother texting back.

I knocked on the glass wall as I stepped into Martha's office. "Hi, I wanted to get the information for the party. Paul mentioned that you'd have it."

"It's on your calendar, and I included the address. The party starts at six. Dinner is included. Dress is festive."

My brain raced to store the information. "Festive?"

Her lips curled into a smile. "A suit with a brightly colored tie would work well. Women wear holiday dresses. Cocktail dresses or Christmas themed."

"Thanks." Instead of walking back to my office, which would have been the safe thing to do, I leaned on the edge of her desk. "This is the first time I've had a job where I was invited to the partner's holiday party. I feel a little out of my depth."

As she stood, she slipped a soft peppermint into my hand. "You'll do fine. Be yourself."

"If I send you pictures of my ties, could you—never mind. That would probably be weird."

She let the tips of her fingers skim my hand. "I'm happy to help you choose a tie."

"The only one I have that's festive is one that is striped

like a candy cane. My sister bought it for me because of my abnormal love of all things peppermint."

Martha fiddled with papers on her desk, lining up the corners. "I think that would look very nice with a dark suit."

"Thank you. I was nervous about taking this job, but you've been a huge help." I inched backward, reminding myself that kissing her would lose me the job and might endanger hers too. "I appreciate all that you've done."

"And I appreciate what you did for me. The night we met, you saved me from embarrassing myself any more than I did, and you made sure I arrived home safely. You're one of the good ones."

Telling my sister that I wanted a woman with bright green eyes and hair that looked light brown when she was indoors at night and blonde when the sun danced in her hair would only stir more questions.

Martha cleared her throat. "Did you get my note about not being in the office tomorrow?"

"Yes, I'm not looking forward to braving the office on my own, but I hope you have a good day."

"If you need anything, Rita can help you. She works as the assistant to James."

"Thanks." I moved away from her desk, wishing I could think of some reason to extend the conversation.

"If you change your mind about the tie, feel free to text me." Martha picked up her purse. "Um, I . . . I need to tell you something, but I don't want it to affect our working relationship."

I stepped closer. "Of course."

She blew out a breath. "My dad—"

James stuck his head in the door. "I hate to interrupt, but could I speak with you for a moment, Owen?"

I shot a glance at Martha.

"I'll see you later." She hooked her purse on her shoulder.

Whatever she was going to tell me would have to wait. The weekend suddenly seemed long.

Saturday evening, wearing my peppermint-striped tie, I knocked at my sister's apartment door. Thankfully, Lia's roommate had agreed to be my date for the evening. I'd spent most of the day trying to remember what she looked like.

Lia opened the door. "Your invitation was so appealing to my friends, I thought I'd have to go with you."

"Look, I don't want anyone getting the wrong idea. I was trying to be clear."

"What's her name?"

"Rory, right?" I'd repeated it to myself over and over as I drove so I wouldn't forget.

"I don't mean my roommate."

"If I were dating someone else, I wouldn't have asked you to help me find a date." I checked the time. "We need to go. I don't want to be late."

"Rory, he's here."

A petite blonde walked out wearing a plum-colored cocktail dress. She flashed a shy smile. "Hi."

"Thanks for going with me tonight."

Lia rolled her eyes. "Just go."

Rory walked out, and I followed.

Lia caught my sleeve. "Next time, you should coordinate your tie to what your date is wearing. Too late for that now."

"Then why say something?" Now I had one more thing to worry about.

She flashed her little sister smile. "Have fun."

CHAPTER 12

MARTHA

Mom stepped out of the way of the waiters. "Everything is ready. Thank you so much for helping me yesterday. It looks fabulous."

"It'll be great." I smoothed my dress, questioning my choice.

"The red and white combination is perfect on you. You look like a peppermint princess." Mom turned when Dad walked down the stairs, then swung back around. "I found the perfect game for tonight. Remember that old movie Charade? The game they play where they pass the orange? I thought that would be a fun activity."

I tried to imagine passing the orange to Owen. "I'm sure the guests will love it."

"I need you to participate." She waggled her finger. "Seriously. All it takes are a few volunteers to get it going."

"Yes, ma'am."

Guests trickled in, and I stayed out of the way, watching but trying not to be seen. The library doorway offered the perfect spot to observe from a distance.

When Owen walked in with a pretty blonde on his arm,

my stomach soured. My eyes were probably glowing green with jealousy. I could probably sneak upstairs and spend the evening with my sister Bella. She never came down during fancy parties.

Dad walked toward the library. "There you are. Join the guests. Owen just arrived."

Yippee.

With my stomach fluttering, I regretted not eating earlier in the day. Tonight, I wasn't sure I could make myself eat.

"I was just about to head out there."

"You aren't a good liar." Dad held out his arm.

I looped my arm around his. "I'm going out there." In only a few seconds, Owen would know that the Morgan half of Morgan and Steiner was my father.

We stepped into the living room, and Dad walked us right up to Owen.

"So glad you could make it." Dad extended his hand to Owen's date. "Paul Morgan and this is my daughter Martha."

"Rory Lewis." The woman on Owen's arm smiled.

Owen smiled and met my gaze. His jaw tightened for a split second. Was he mad? "Good evening. You have a lovely home, Paul. The whole place is very festive. It looks great."

"My wife and Martha are to thank for that. They spent all day yesterday decorating for the party."

Rory scanned the room. "It's beautiful."

"Thank you. The buffet is open in the dining room and the bar is over there." I pointed to the different areas.

"I'll leave y'all to talk." Dad walked away.

Owen rubbed his whiskers, which he did when he was nervous. "Which way? Food or drink?"

Rory leaned closer to me. "Where can I find the ladies' room?"

"Down the hall. First door on the right."

She patted Owen's arm. "I'll be right back."

When she was out of earshot, he stepped closer to me. "Is this what you were going to say when we got interrupted?" Owen kept his voice low and stood close. Too close.

"Yes. I didn't want you to be caught off guard. I don't always say anything because I like to be judged on the work I do, not on who my father is."

"Does he know?"

"About what?"

"Last weekend."

I glanced around to make sure no one was close enough to hear. "Are you kidding? No!"

Staring at the rug, he inched closer. "You look beautiful tonight." He said it without looking at me.

"Thank you. I'd already planned to wear this when you mentioned the tie. I didn't choose it because of that." I needed to walk away; I just didn't want to. "If you need anything this evening, I'll be around."

"Martha." Now, he focused those baby blues on me. "I understand, and it won't change anything."

"Good. When Rory comes back, you should get food. The caterer is amazing. You'll love the options."

He motioned to the decorations. "Have you eaten today?"

I shook my head. "But I'm not sure I could eat anything right now. And I definitely don't plan on drinking."

Rory made her way through the crowd.

"I'll give you time with your date." I started to step away.

Owen touched my arm. "She's my sister's roommate and came with me as a favor to my sister. I had a bit of trouble finding a date."

None of that information did anything to tamp down the jealousy bubbling in my chest. "I hope you have a nice evening." If I didn't slip away now, I'd say something that would haunt me.

For the better part of an hour, I stayed away from Owen.

Other than catching him watching me from across the room, nothing happened between us until Mom gathered everyone for the game.

"I need people to line up in two lines. Boy. Girl. Boy. Girl. And I need two volunteers to help me demonstrate."

Owen was standing a little too close to my mom, and when she spotted his red and white tie, he was doomed.

Mom clasped his arm. "Remind me of your name again. I'm sorry."

"Owen."

"Owen, will you help me demonstrate?"

"Sure." He sounded completely unsure.

"Martha, you are nicely coordinated with Owen. Come help me." I wasn't sure if my mom sensed something or just had the worst ideas and timing.

I stepped to the front, horrified by what she was about to ask us to do and thrilled that I would get to do it with Owen.

She beamed, excited about her idea. "This will be a race. There will be two teams. I'll hand the orange to the person at the front of each line, and they have to pass it to the next person. No one can touch the orange with their hands. Owen and Martha will demonstrate." She tucked an orange under Owen's chin. "Pass that to Martha."

He inched closer, his gaze locked on mine.

I nodded, giving him permission to get close.

His hands moved to my hips, and we pressed our bodies against each other. With my head tilted one way and his tilted the opposite way, we worked to get the orange under my chin. In the movie, the game offered challenges. Demonstrating the game also offered challenges. The orange rolled down his chest, and I had to chase it. Thankfully, I managed to snag it before it moved embarrassingly low. As I made sure the orange was trapped under my chin, I glanced up at Owen. That was a mistake. I nearly dropped the orange.

When I stepped away from him, he jumped back and rubbed the back of his neck.

"Bravo!" My mom had been watching too many old movies. "Does everyone understand?"

The crowd nodded and lined up.

Mom pushed Owen and I toward the back of one line. "They need two more people."

"Where's Rory?" I didn't want to ruin the poor woman's night.

"Right here." The smile she flashed me made me not want to drink out of anything I'd left unattended.

"You two get in that line. I'll watch." I moved out of the way.

Mom counted the teams. Standing next to Owen, she motioned to me. "This side needs one more person."

I dutifully moved into place.

The game drew laughter from the crowd, and I didn't even want to think about what pictures would be posted online.

Watching Rory pass the orange to Owen was the hardest part of the evening. The way her hands moved on his back, I was certain her plans for the night and his didn't match at all.

Why was I so jealous? I couldn't date him.

Owen whipped around with the orange tucked under his chin. Both teams shouted as the orange passed to the last couple on the other team. We were vying for the win.

Fueled by a competitive spirit and something else I wouldn't admit to, I pressed in close, wrapping my arms around him. "I had no idea we'd end up this way."

"Your hair smells like peppermint." His lips brushed my neck, and I nearly dropped the orange. Again.

"Focus on the orange."

"I'm trying." His arms tightened around me. "I really am."

With all the cheering and yelling, I doubted our whispers

could be heard. The orange rolled halfway down his chest again. It wasn't like I was letting it roll down on purpose. I hugged him around the middle as I worked to trap the orange.

"Hurry." Owen's breath on my ear did not help me.

I snagged the orange. "I'm so sorry about this."

He pulled back as I took control of the orange. "I'm not."

I lifted my arms, and our team went wild. Everyone except Rory. She tapped Owen's arm and pointed toward the door.

He nodded. "I need to go. I'll talk to you later."

"Bye."

He said a quick goodbye to my dad before escorting Rory out the door.

I had to hang out for another hour until the rest of the guests left even though I wanted to go home and indulge in a good cry. I hated the company policy.

CHAPTER 13

OWEN

Rory was silent as I drove her home. When I walked her to the door, I apologized because that seemed like the right thing to do. But I wasn't completely clear about why she was mad.

She nodded and walked inside.

I trudged back down to my car. After buckling in, I counted. One. Two. Three. Four. My phone rang.

"Hey, Lia."

"What did you do?"

"I didn't do anything. I think maybe she misunderstood about it not being a real date."

"She said you were flirting with someone else at the party."

"I was not flirting with Martha. She's my admin assistant." I spit out the words with conviction.

Lia laughed. "Ooooh. Your personal assistant. I don't get you, Owen. Why didn't you just take her to the party?"

"There are rules, Lia. In the grown-up world, there are rules."

She hung up on me, which I probably deserved.

Frustrated with myself and wishing I could have asked Martha several other questions, I ran home to change, then stopped at the store and bought the ingredients for the brownie dessert she'd served the other night. I also bought a cooler and dry ice. I wasn't sure how long it would be before Martha returned home.

I drove to her house and parked in front. It didn't matter how long I had to wait, I wasn't going to find a solution to our problem. There wasn't one. Not a good one anyway.

And knowing her dad was a partner only complicated things further.

When the garage door lifted, and her car pulled into the garage, I grabbed the cooler. Before I climbed out of the car, a message popped up.

Pull in the driveway. It's less suspicious.

There was a benefit to driving the same make, model, and color of car that she drove.

The front door opened when I stepped onto the porch.

"Why are you here?" The smile on her face softened the accusation buried in the question, but only a little.

I lifted the cooler. "I brought all the stuff for dessert and thought that if you haven't eaten, we could order a pizza."

She stepped aside. "You didn't answer the question."

I dragged my fingers through my hair. "Your dad told you I'd been hired and that Bob was leaving."

"He did. We don't talk much about work, but occasionally he tells me things."

"That's why you knew my name and that I'd be at the party." I forced myself not to inch closer.

"Yes." She glanced down at the cooler. "I haven't eaten."

"I'll order the pizza."

She walked toward the hall, then stopped. "I feel bad that Rory was upset."

"Me too. Everything would be so much easier if . . ."

Martha shook her head. "We can't, Owen. I've worked at this company since I was in college. I like my job. And flaunting the rules would shed a bad light on my dad. I won't do that."

"I'm not asking you to. Really." I felt guilty even saying it. "Do you want me to leave?"

"I'll be out in a minute or two. Pepperoni sounds good."

I ordered the pizza, kicking myself for venting . . . and for coming.

Martha walked back out, wearing candy cane pajamas. She sat at the opposite end of the sofa. "I had no idea my mother would put us on the spot like that. I felt bad for your date."

"Now I feel even worse. I didn't mean for anyone's feelings to be hurt."

She smiled, and somewhere an angel probably earned its wings. "I am glad you came over."

"This is the last time."

"That's probably a good idea." She picked up the remote. "Want to watch a movie?"

"Sure."

She turned on an old film starring Cary Grant and Audrey Hepburn.

"I expected something Christmas themed."

"I felt like watching this one." She tucked her feet up beside her.

We paused it when the pizza arrived, then ate during the second half of the movie. By the end, we were both on the floor next to each other.

She sighed. "I love that ending."

"We watched this because of the game, didn't we?"

"It's where Mom got the idea."

"Let me make dessert, then after we indulge, I'll go."

As I stood, she grabbed my hand. "I haven't said it, but I do wish things were different."

I gave into impulse and kissed her fingers. "I know."

I'd known her one week, and I was trying to figure out how to cram my feelings back into a dark corner of my heart.

~

MONDAY MORNING, I didn't buy Martha a cup of her favorite chai tea.

She showed up and acted like we'd never socialized outside of the office. It should've made work easier, but for me, it was harder than last week.

My phone rang, and I answered. "Hi, Lia. What's up?"

"Want to grab lunch?" She'd never called me out of the blue, asking about lunch.

After the debacle with her roommate, I decided lunch might be an easy way to smooth things over. "Sure. Where do you want me to meet you?"

"We'll come up to your office."

"We?"

"Rory is with me." Lia hung up.

I poked my head into Martha's office. "My sister is coming up to meet me for lunch. I'll be out of the office for about an hour."

"All right." She flashed that big beautiful smile.

Ten minutes later, when Rory and Lia walked into my office, Martha was no longer smiling. I felt awful.

"We should go." I led the ladies out to the elevator. "Let's find something close. I need to be back here in an hour." As the doors opened, I remembered that my wallet was sitting in my desk drawer. "Y'all go down. I'll meet you in the lobby."

I walked into Martha's office and closed her door. "I'm

not dating Rory. She just showed up with my sister. If this is uncomfortable for you, I can—"

"Not at all." She didn't look up as she said it.

I hated that phrase.

She tapped away at her keyboard. "They're waiting. Did you need anything else?"

"I'll be back in an hour." I grabbed my wallet and headed downstairs.

Lia crossed her arms as I walked outside, and Rory laughed.

I didn't feel like eating.

"What? Hop in. Y'all can berate me as I drive." I opened the front and back doors for them.

As soon as I pulled out of the parking lot, Rory spoke. "I was mad because I thought you'd invited me to make that woman jealous. Coming up to your office proved insightful."

I hated when women used words like insightful. "I wasn't trying to make anyone jealous. The partner said to bring a date. So I asked Lia for help."

Lia rubbed my arm. "Rory pointed out the one that has you lovesick. She works for you, huh?"

"Yes. I already told you she was my admin assistant. But it doesn't matter where in the company she works. There is a strict no-dating policy. And for the record, I'm not lovesick."

Peals of laughter echoed in the car.

"I wasn't trying to be funny."

Rory subdued her laughter first. "Owen, it's pretty clear that you're nuts about her."

I glanced into the rearview mirror, and she nodded when she met my gaze. If they could tell, could everyone? "Is it that obvious?"

"Only to people watching." Lia's comment wasn't all that helpful.

"I'm the new guy. Everyone is watching me."

CHAPTER 14

MARTHA

Friday morning, I stood in my closet, not feeling festive and trying to decide what to wear. Since I'd taken off last Friday to help Mom, I hadn't worn my elf dress. Should I wear that or the sugarplum dress? The elf dress jingled. Maybe a day full of jingle bells would put me in a better mood.

The week had been much more difficult than I'd anticipated. Seeing Owen go to lunch with Rory had my insides in knots.

I pulled the elf costume off the hanger.

If I could make it through today, I wouldn't see Owen again until next year. It sounded like a long time, and my heart ached at the thought.

But distance was good.

After getting dressed, as I stuffed silver dollar pancakes into a baggie—I'd found something to do when I couldn't sleep—my phone buzzed. Why was my sister texting so early?

You should quit your job and date the hottie. She was fifteen. What did she know?

I tapped out a quick reply that would hopefully end the discussion. *Thanks for the advice, but I like paying my mortgage and eating.*

The phone rang.

"What?" I shoved the baggie into my purse.

"First of all, you don't owe anything on that house. Second of all, you can find another job, but guys like him don't come along every day." She sounded chipper, if not a bit dictatorial, for this early in the morning.

"You didn't even come downstairs during the party. And I never said I liked him."

"I came down for the game. That was hilarious, by the way. And if you want the video of Owen passing you the orange, let me know. I didn't post it anywhere. But clearly, y'all have a thing." She took video?

"We don't have a thing." I wanted to have a thing, but that was out of the question. "I need to go. I'll talk to you later."

"We still going shopping tomorrow?" For a little sister, Bella wasn't so bad.

"Yes, I'll take you shopping." I dropped my phone into my purse and hurried out the door.

When I parked outside the office, a familiar car was already there. I jingled my way toward the elevators, watching them closely. At the last second, they opened again.

I swallowed the lump in my throat and plastered on a smile as I stepped into the elevator.

Owen stood in the corner with his arms crossed. "Good morning. I heard the jingling and knew . . . it had to be you."

And now I would have a song playing on repeat in my head. "Thanks for holding the elevator."

"After you get settled, I'd like to speak with you . . . if you have time."

"Sure."

I took my time getting settled—as he put it—before

walking into his office. I had that awful sense that I was not going to like the conversation.

"What did you need?"

He let his gaze drift down my green and red dress. Then he scrubbed his face. "Because of the unique circumstances in our situation it seems that working with me is stressful for you. I don't like seeing you upset." He paced back and forth behind his desk, dragging his fingers through his hair. "So I was thinking—I haven't yet mentioned this to anyone else—it might be good if you and Rita switched. She could be my admin, and you could work for James. It's a lateral move. It won't affect your pay." Panic swirled in his blue eyes. "What do you think?"

I refused to cry. "I'll start packing my office."

"Do you think it's a bad idea?"

"Not at all." I closed the door between our offices, then pushed the button on the wall to close the blinds. "I'll be in my office if you need anything."

"Martha."

I stopped in his office doorway, and after a deep breath I turned around. "Yes?"

"Do you have a better idea? Because if you do, please tell me."

"I don't." I closed myself in my office, ordered boxes to be delivered, and set to work dismantling my workspace.

CHAPTER 15

OWEN

A continuous jingling sounded in the office next door. Martha hadn't stopped moving since walking out of my office.

Even as dense as I was, I knew she wasn't happy about my suggestion, but in the long run, it would be best. I hoped so.

James poked his head in the door. "You wanted to see me?"

"Come in and close the door."

He dropped into a chair and furrowed his brow when he noticed that the blinds were closed. "I haven't seen those closed since your first day."

"I think it might be best—and I've already suggested this to Martha—that we switch admins. Would that be okay with you?"

James dropped his head into his hands. When he finally looked at me, he blew out an exasperated breath. "May I speak freely?"

"Of course." I really wanted a simple yes or no, not a lecture.

"You have a funny way of showing someone how much you care about them."

"What?"

"How could you do that to her? She's great at her job, and while I'd love working with her, I would never be party to embarrassing her in that way." He stood and moved closer.

I flashed back to when he towered over me in the doorway at the venue, and a lot of other memories came with it. I wasn't exactly short, but this guy was like a wall. Stepping back, I grabbed the back of my chair. "Embarrass her? I'm not trying to embarrass her. Why would you say that?"

James leaned forward, getting right in my face. "There is a pecking order. Pay scales are important, but so are perceptions. There's an admin for the big boss and an admin for the little boss. Do you see what I'm getting at?"

I sank into my chair. "I messed up."

"Big time."

"And I do care. That's the problem."

"Breaking her heart is not the solution." James walked toward the door. "I'll go so you can figure out how to fix things."

The door closed, and I pushed the button to open the blinds. Her Christmas tree was already bare. Half-filled boxes were scattered on the floor.

I knocked before stepping into her office through our private door.

She turned and stared before motioning me in. Her mascara was perfect. There was no hint that she'd been crying.

I took one step toward her but stopped when she stepped back.

"What do you need?" She crossed her arms.

"I don't want to switch admins. It hadn't occurred to me

that it would shed a bad light on you. So, please, just put everything back."

"I'm not sure I can do that. Steiner has asked me more than once to be his admin, so I'll move to his office. You can hire someone to fill my spot."

I played her words in my head, trying to make sense of it all. "I thought Steiner was dead."

"His son stepped in as partner when his dad died." She squeezed the tissue wadded up in her hand. "Is there anything else?"

"I don't want you to leave. I want you . . . to be happy, but I think I ruined that."

"Once I finish packing, I'll have maintenance guys move everything to my dad's office until I get details sorted out. Since I won't be back until after New Year's, I don't want to leave the office cluttered with stuff." She pinched her lips, and her quivering chin knotted my stomach.

"I'm sorry." I shoved my hands in my pockets to stop me from pulling her into my arms. "And don't move anything. We'll figure it out when you get back. Please."

She nodded. "Sure. But I'm going to take the rest of the day off."

"Whatever you need. I feel like I've robbed you of Christmas cheer."

A single tear slipped down her cheek. "Maybe a little." Without looking at me, she picked up her purse and hurried out of the office.

I was the worst Grinch of all.

But I didn't mean to be.

One thing Martha said poked at my brain. Steiner. If he'd wanted her to be his admin, why hadn't she made the switch earlier? It wasn't hard to tell she wasn't a fan of Bob.

I needed answers, and I needed someone who would spill the whole truth. "Liza, may I speak with you?"

She bounced into the office and dropped into a chair. "What's up with the boxes in Martha's office?"

"I don't want to talk about that."

"Lovers' quarrel, huh? I haven't turned y'all in, just so you know."

This day was only getting worse. "Nothing is going on. Tell me about Steiner."

"The dead one or the handsy one?"

Now I was going to be sick. "Never mind. I think I've heard enough. And Martha and I are not dating."

"Maybe you should be." Liza crossed her arms. "Okay, so here's the thing. I'm not Martha's biggest fan. She works her tail off when she could just play the my-dad-is-a-partner card. That makes no sense to me. And I didn't mean to get her drunk. I just wanted her to relax a little. How was I supposed to know she hadn't eaten and never drank? Anyway, I'm not sure what I was trying to say. Apparently, you like all those quirky things about her." She rubbed her forehead. "Is that all?"

"Yes, Liza. That's all." I dialed Mr. Morgan's secretary, hoping I could grab a spot on his calendar before he left for the holidays.

CHAPTER 16

MARTHA

Instead of going down to my car, I rode the elevator to the top floor. As much as I hated the idea of working for Brad Steiner, it would get me away from Owen, and right now, I wanted that more than anything.

I stepped off the elevator and bumped into my father. Bad timing on a bad day.

"Hey, sweetheart, what are you doing up here?" He glanced at his phone when it buzzed.

Lying was pointless because he'd know within an hour. "I'm going to chat with Steiner about transferring."

"Let's have lunch." Dad pointed into the elevator as the doors opened.

I'd expected a furrowed brow, not a lunch invitation. "All right."

Once we were on the way to the restaurant, he spoke again. "What has you so upset that you'd even consider working for Brad? I know how you feel about him. Is Owen really that bad?"

"No. That's not it. Owen isn't bad at all. I do *not* want you to think that." My answer came out too shrill and too quick.

Dad laughed. "I'm not sure working for Brad is the solution."

"He's not horrible. He just . . ." I'd known Brad from the time I could walk. "He's just touchy-feely, not in a creepy way, but I don't have to explain it to you. You know."

"I know you wouldn't be happy working for him. And, sweetheart, I want you to be happy."

I'd heard that before, minus the sweetheart part. "I know."

"Wait until after Christmas. Then make a decision. But don't say anything to Brad before that." Did Dad know something I didn't?

"Owen said the same thing. Have you talked to him?"

"I have not. In fact, I don't think I've seen Owen since the party on Saturday. Did he enjoy himself?"

"I think so." I closed my eyes and was back at the party playing that game, more aware of Owen's hands on me than that stupid orange.

Dad shifted the car into park. "I like that guy."

Right now, that didn't make me feel any better. I choked back the 'I do too' that begged to be said.

CHAPTER 17

OWEN

*A*t four in the afternoon, James knocked. "The office cleared out early today. I'm headed out, but I'll be in on Monday and Tuesday."

"Thanks for your help."

"I hope everything works out." He motioned toward Martha's office. "With . . . you know."

"Yes, I know exactly what you mean. Have a great weekend." I stayed in my chair until I heard the main doors close, then I grabbed an unused box from beside Martha's desk and packed up the few items I'd brought to the office.

By four-thirty, I was ready for my meeting.

Mr. Morgan was seated at his desk when I knocked. "Come in, Owen. Have a seat."

"I didn't mean to keep you late today, sir. This should only take a few minutes."

He leaned back in his chair. "What's on your mind?"

I'd spent hours trying to decide what to say, but at the moment, my main goal was to not make a fool of myself. After circling the chair twice, I sat down. "I'm crazy about your daughter. The night of their department Christmas party, someone gave her spiked punch."

Mr. Morgan leaned forward, anger burning in his eyes.

"When I realized it, I made sure it didn't happen anymore, and I kept her next to me because she was tipsy, and I didn't want anything to happen. But she mistook me for the Santa she'd hired. I am completely mixing up this story."

"Please continue."

"She mentioned that her parents were out of town, and I didn't feel right leaving her alone, so I slept on her living room floor. Then on Sunday instead of taking her directly to pick up her car, I spent the entire day with her shopping at Christmas stores and looking at lights in the Hill Country."

"We will circle back to the part about spiked punch in a bit. But what's the problem?"

"The policy." I didn't expect him to give me an exemption, but I could hope.

"Would you like to know why we have that policy?"

I didn't care why they had the policy. I cared that it was tearing me up and making Martha cry. But I wasn't about to say that to her father. "Why?"

"Years ago, Brett Steiner and I had a great idea, and we started a business. When we'd grown enough to hire people, he interviewed secretaries until he found a beautiful candidate. He hired her on the spot." Paul Morgan closed his eyes and smiled.

I waited while the man remembered.

"She'd just moved from Houston. She was efficient and delightful to work with. Smart, too. Because she was new and didn't know many people, I took her to lunch most days. Then after a month, I asked her out. Brett was furious. A month after we started dating, he showed up with the new policy and threatened to quit if I didn't agree to it. I read over it, then asked for a week to think about it. He let me do that."

"Obviously you signed it." I wanted to know the reason for the long story.

"I did. But you know what is not in our corporate policy?"

"What's that?"

"Rules against nepotism. Before I said yes to Brett, I talked to Nancy, the beautiful secretary. By the time I signed off on that policy, I was married to her."

That was a solution I hadn't thought of. "I haven't even kissed Martha. Well, she kissed me when she was tipsy, but—"

"Don't finish that sentence. I don't want to know." He shook his head. "I kept the dating policy in place after Brett died because of his son. Brad has liked Martha since the first grade. As long as they both worked at the company and there was a strict policy in place, I didn't have to worry about him asking her out."

"You don't like him?" I wasn't sure I ever wanted to meet Brad Steiner.

"I just don't like him for my daughter. Now, back to your problem. Do you have a better idea?"

I pulled the folded resignation letter out of my pocket. "This. But I'll only resign on one condition."

"You realize how ridiculous that sounds, right?"

"I do, Mr. Morgan, I mean, Paul, but I should never have been hired. James deserves this job. When I suggested to Martha today that she switch jobs with Rita—"

"You did what?"

I inched my chair backward. "James explained why that was a horrible idea. But I'd already hurt her feelings. I can't let her go work for someone she doesn't like. I already feel like I've ruined her Christmas. And it makes me sick."

"I can see why because she loves Christmas."

"Will you accept my resignation and my terms?"

He stood and rested his knuckles on the desk. "Let me get

this straight. You are going to quit your job so that you can ask my daughter out?"

"Yes, sir. And hopefully you don't have a problem with your daughter dating someone who is unemployed."

He dropped back into his chair. "I will accept your resignation and hire James on one condition."

"Anything." I'd figured out a solution. My only hope now was that Martha could forgive me.

CHAPTER 18

MARTHA

I'd picked up Bella, and sweet sister that she was, she spent the afternoon with me.

At six, she sprang up off the couch. "Time to go. Dinner is in a half hour, and being late is unacceptable."

"I really don't feel like dinner. I'll just drop you off."

"Nope. You know that's not an option. Daddy wants to see his girls to make sure they are happy." My sister's second language was sarcasm.

"He cares, and you don't have to tell me what Dad wants. He bought me a house and gave me a job so that I'd stay in town. I know how much he likes having us close."

"I'm not playing that game." Bella propped her hands on her hips. "I won't let him buy me a house. And I will not go to work for his company either."

"You say that now."

"I mean it. Now, let's go before I get in trouble for making us late." She wasn't wrong about that. As the baby, she got more than her fair share of blame.

"I don't want to get you in trouble. I've caused enough of that already."

We drove to the house and went directly to the dining room. It was empty, but there were five place settings on the table.

"Where are Mom and Dad and who else is eating dinner with us?"

Bella shrugged. "Don't ask me. I was with you all afternoon." She held out her phone. "While we're waiting, do you want to watch that video?"

"Of course not—give me the phone. Which one did you video?"

"Both of them. I put them into one video, then added some music."

I tapped the play button and Harry Connick, Jr. started singing "It Had to Be You." I'd made it almost through our demonstration when I stopped the video. "I can't finish this. It's making me sad."

She hugged me. "I'm sorry."

"Let's go find Mom."

We didn't even make it to the door before Mom sashayed into the dining room.

"Your father will be here soon. He had to meet with someone because something happened at work. I'm not sure of all the details." She grinned. "But tonight I decided to go casual. We're having Thai food from your favorite place."

"Thanks, Mom. That sounds great." My news had traveled.

I sat down, folded my arms, and buried my face. I stayed that way while bags crinkled and after I heard Dad's voice announcing he was home. But when Bella kicked me under the table, I glanced up. "What?"

Dad smiled. "Feeling any better?"

"I bought her favorite. That might cheer her up." Mom gave him one of those looks that said she knew something I didn't.

"I know what will cheer her up." Dad scratched his chin.

Was I supposed to guess?

Bella's eyes widened and she kicked me again.

"What?"

"Behind you."

I looked over my shoulder.

Owen stood in the doorway. "Hi. I quit my job today."

My chair fell over when I launched at him.

"Mistletoe is in the living room. I do not want to watch." Dad chuckled. "And stay away from the oranges."

Owen tugged me toward the living room. "I'm sorry about asking you to—"

"I can't believe you're here."

Smiling down at me, he brushed his thumb across my lower lip. "Ever since you kissed me in the men's room, I've wanted to kiss you again."

Kissing him and having him kiss me back was near the top of my Christmas wish list.

He crushed me against him as his lips met mine.

And oh did he kiss me back.

When I pulled away, he trailed a knuckle down my cheek. "Will you go out with me?" Did he really have to ask?

"You seriously quit your job? I feel bad that you gave up your big career opportunity for me."

"After I informed your dad, he met with James. He will be taking over as department head."

I cradled Owen's face. "You're amazing."

"Do you have any brownies?"

I slid my arms around his neck. "I have all the ingredients. All I need is someone to keep me company while I bake."

He dotted kisses on my face. "I know someone who is definitely interested. And tomorrow, we can spend all day together."

"I'm taking Bella shopping."

"Mom can take me." Bella laughed, then ran back to the dining room.

Owen pulled me closer. "Looks like you're free."

"I can't believe you quit your job."

He rubbed a hand up and down my back, grinning. "I thought about you constantly. That makes it hard to work. Then you looked so sad when Rory showed up at the office and you looked so cute in that elf dress with the little jingle bells." He threaded his fingers into my hair and pulled me to his lips. Still kissing me, he lifted me into his arms. "I can find another job, but I'm pretty sure that finding someone who loves Christmas as much as you do is impossible. When I take you to dinner tomorrow night, will you wear that peppermint dress?"

I nodded.

"And the night after that, when I take you to dinner, you can wear the sugarplum dress I haven't gotten to see."

My cheeks burned, and I knew they were red.

"We should probably go back to the table. I want your parents to like me."

After he put me down, I laced my fingers with his. "I think what's really important is that I like you. A lot."

"Merry Christmas to me."

AFTER SPENDING MOST of every day with Owen, I sipped tea before heading to my parents' house on Christmas morning. Having a teenage sister meant I got to sleep in a little. Breakfast was at ten; gifts followed.

I changed into my Mrs. Claus onesie and headed to the house. Our family tradition had always been to wear pajamas on Christmas morning. And I loved it.

When I walked into my parents' house, the smell of

cinnamon greeted me. "Breakfast smells good. What are we having?"

Mom wrapped me in a hug. "The crème brûlée French toast from that cookbook I love. But I added cinnamon."

"I love that. I can't wait. Is Bella up?"

"She's been up for hours. I can't figure that girl out." Mom laughed. "But we did have fun shopping last weekend. We haven't seen much of you. I'm guessing you've been spending time with Owen."

"Almost every waking minute."

"Is he joining us this morning?"

I shook my head. "I think maybe he was going to drive to Houston. He didn't say. He just said he had a thing this morning. Maybe he didn't want to crash our family Christmas." I washed my hands, then rubbed them together as Mom sprinkled sugar on the top of the French toast. "And I know it's probably way too soon to say this, but I love him."

Mom laughed. "You know my story, so I won't give you a hard time. I think sometimes you just know." She handed me the butane torch. "Go ahead. I know you want to make that sugar turn to glass."

I torched the top, careful not to burn the sugar. Watching it bubble, then turn shiny had always been entertaining. "I think that's good."

"Time to eat!" Mom carried the dish to the table.

And I was glad I wasn't the one carrying it when I walked into the dining room and saw my favorite Santa on one knee.

"Martha Morgan, will you make me the jolliest Santa ever and marry me?"

"Yes!" I threw my arms around his neck.

He managed to stand up with me clinging to him. His breath tickled my ear as he spoke. "As soon as I get a job, I'll buy you a ring. But I didn't want to wait because all I want for Christmas—and every day after that—is you."

"Owen Reynolds, you are proposing to me in a Santa costume on Christmas day. I can't imagine anything more romantic. *You* are what I want."

"I thought maybe we'd have a Christmas-themed wedding . . . in July." He winked.

My mind raced with all the decorating possibilities. "I love that idea."

"Merry Christmas, Martha." My Santa kissed me until my toes curled.

And he tasted like peppermint.

EPILOGUE

OWEN

TEN YEARS LATER

I snuggled up next to Martha on the sofa. Christmas lights twinkled on the Christmas tree, and holiday music played quietly through a small speaker. "Both kids are sound asleep. Natalie will probably be up at the crack of dawn. Then Nathan will hear her and demand to be out of his crib."

Martha leaned her head on my shoulder. "That's the fun of Christmas." She shifted, then pulled my arms around her so that my hand rested on her belly. "Are you excited?"

"Very. And a little nervous. We're moving from man-to-man to zone defense. It's a different set of skills." I'd spent years thinking that life couldn't get any better after meeting Martha. Then I became a dad. Adding a third kid to the mix would make life even more interesting and full of love.

"I hadn't even thought of it that way."

I'd loved Martha, but seeing her as a mom bumped that to

a whole new level. I kissed the top of her head. "Feeling okay?"

"Mostly. If I stay far away from the orange juice." She laughed, then sighed. "I'm a little concerned about how Dad will take our other news."

I'd spent the last week worrying about the same thing. "You and me both. When I met with him that Friday afternoon ten years ago, I put conditions on my resignation. He put one condition on accepting it."

She sat up. "You never told me that."

"It didn't seem necessary. Until recently." I pulled her back against me. "He said that he'd accept my resignation if I promised never to look for a job in a different city. He meant that he wanted me to stay in Austin, but that wasn't what he said."

"You're going to hold him to his technicality?"

"I am. This job transfer wasn't my idea. It's a good job, and I like it. But if I want to keep it, we have to move." I buried my face in the curve of her neck. "I didn't go looking for a job in a different city."

"Dad is a reasonable man. He'll understand." Martha didn't sound as hopeful as her words would imply.

Dropping kisses along her neck, I laughed. "Your dad doesn't want his girls to move away from him. And I'm going to be the bad guy that makes that happen."

"It'll all work out." She tilted her head back. "Are you going to put on the Santa suit and tuck the presents under the tree?"

"I thought we were opening gifts at your parents' house."

"We are, but I have a couple small things for the kids to open first thing."

"You just want me to put on the Santa suit."

She shifted and straddled my lap. "Always. And don't bother buttoning the coat."

A NOTE TO READERS

Thank you for reading! Martha and Owen came to life as I wrote Bella's story, *Christmas Sparkle*. In the beginning, all I knew was the Martha seriously loved Christmas.

I had fun with this story. I hope it made you laugh and smile.

CHRISTMAS SPARKLE

Her most embarrassing moment leads to the best Christmas ever.

CHAPTER 1

BELLA

I yanked my sundress out of the dryer with one hand, trying to calm my nephew with the other. Static crackled. I should have used a dryer sheet, but my sister was so organized I couldn't find a thing. They were probably in a cabinet in a labeled bin, but who had time to hunt through cabinets when pandemonium reigned?

My nephew rubbed his eyes and continued to cry. Most of his time was spent eating, pooping, or crying. Were all seven-month-olds this way? No wonder my sister needed a break.

"Shhh, Nathan. I'll look for your blanket in a minute." I slammed the dryer shut and carried my wadded dress toward the stairs. As soon as my sister walked through the door, I was leaving.

Kids were wonderful but exhausting. My good deed had zapped me of every last ounce of energy.

Nathan pounded on my shoulder, sobbing. If the blanket was so important to him, why did he keep dropping it everywhere?

"Natalie, are you almost ready?" I peeked into my niece's

room.

She twirled in her princess dress. "I can't find my sparkly panties." She said it as if I was supposed to know which pair she meant.

I'd been here two days. In all that time, I had not taken the time to inventory her underwear drawer. "Wear a different pair. They might be in the dryer." I didn't care which pair she chose, just so long as she wore some. "Have you seen your brother's blanket?"

Singing emanated from her room. So much for getting an answer.

Never again would I volunteer to watch my sister's kids overnight. And the next time my sister sweetly requested that I have the kids ready to go out for dinner, I'd laugh. This took as much energy and patience as the rest of the stay.

And that was no small accomplishment. In less than forty-eight hours, the kids had managed to spit up or spill stuff on everything I'd packed, and I'd had to wash my clothes. Eager to help, Natalie had tossed in her clothes also. Now I had to sort laundry before I could race out the door. I didn't want to end up taking sparkly panties home with me.

Scanning the halls for Nathan's blanket, I answered when my phone rang. "Hello?"

"Yikes. You sound stressed. Still on kid duty?" Daisy was my best friend and could read me by the tone of my voice. It took only a single word.

"Martha should be here in fifteen minutes. Hopefully, before she walks through the door, I'll have time to get my laundry out of the dryer, separate out all that my niece threw in, and get dressed. I might be a few minutes late, but I'll meet you at the restaurant."

"I'll wait. It's not like I have anything better to do." Daisy sighed. "Don't you ever want what she has? The husband, the house, the kids?"

"Not today." I set Nathan in his crib right next to his blanket. "Ask me in a week . . . or a year."

Daisy laughed. "That bad, huh?"

"Yes, it was that bad. Which makes me sound horrible." I ran back to Natalie's room and made sure she was fully dressed. "Put your shoes on, okay?"

"Okay!" Natalie continued to spin.

My sister could deal with that.

With Nathan safely in his crib, I ran back down and tossed clothes into my bag straight from the dryer. Everything would be wrinkled, like the dress tucked under my arm.

I still needed to get dressed. "Get a table. I'll be there as soon as I can."

"Will do. And relax. It's almost over." Daisy laughed. "Almost."

"The good thing is, after the day I've had, it can only get better." I ended the call as Daisy's laughter flowed over the line.

After tossing Natalie's clothes into a basket and stuffing mine into my bag, I ran to the downstairs bathroom. Slightly bigger than a changing stall, that room had a lock on the door, a treasure when I was changing clothes.

With Natalie knocking on the bathroom door, I pulled the dress over my head. What a wrinkled mess! But the big streak of spit up on my shirt necessitated changing. I'd rather look like I rolled out of bed than smell like puke. "I'll be out in a second."

"I can't find my shoes."

"I put them next to your bed." Hadn't I? Hopefully, I hadn't put them in the crib with Nathan.

Worried, I shoved my dirty shirt into my bag, dropped my bag beside the door, and darted up the stairs. There were no sparkly shoes in bed with Nathan. He held his blankie in front of his face, then giggled when he pulled it down. He had his cute moments.

"Come put your shoes on." I set the pair at the top of the stairs. "Your parents will be here any minute."

Natalie ran up the stairs, grinning. Apparently, those were the magic words. "I can put them on by myself."

"Great. Thank you for being a good helper."

"I put Nathan's blanket in his crib. He always drops it, so I took it from him and put it where it was safe."

That explained all the tears.

Keys jingled outside, and I bolted down the stairs, leaving Natalie to put on her other shoe.

Right on time, the front door opened. "We're here!" Martha opened her arms as Natalie ran down the stairs.

Nathan screamed from upstairs. The poor kid felt left out.

"All three of you lived!" Martha laughed as she ran up the stairs.

Owen, my brother-in-law, pressed his hands together. "I cannot thank you enough. It was such a treat to talk to my wife. We had entire conversations. It was amazing."

"You're welcome." I picked up my purse and bag. "I should go. Daisy drove up from San Antonio and is waiting for me at a restaurant."

He stepped out of the way. "I won't keep you from your friend. Martha and I really appreciated the getaway."

I didn't have to ask why.

"Have a great night." I leaned toward the stairs. "Bye, Martha!" Without waiting for an answer, I ran to my Honda and headed to the restaurant.

The stars were smiling on me because I found a spot right next to the door. After parking, I ran inside, smoothing the wrinkles in my dress. Somehow, the rubbing only made the static worse. My dress stuck to my legs in a most unladylike way.

Daisy sprang up off the bench in the waiting area. "You made it."

I'd never been so thankful to see my friend. "I did. You get a table. I'm going to run into the ladies' room and see if I can somehow fix this dress."

She crinkled her nose. "You've got a little static cling going on there."

"A little." I walked into the restroom, happy it was unoccupied. The only solution I could think of was water. That got rid of static, right? After getting my hands wet, I rubbed my legs. Even if I couldn't get the dress to stop sticking to itself, I could stop it from clinging to me.

After achieving mild success, I stepped out and scanned the room. Daisy waved from a booth on the far side of the dining area. I made my way over.

Restaurants were interesting places to people watch. At one table, a woman talked, and the guy across from her looked like he was almost asleep. At the next table over from ours, a man sat alone. I couldn't see his face because he had his back to me, but he had a nice line to his shoulders.

As I passed his booth, I wondered how he looked from the front. Just when I contemplated stealing a look, something brushed my leg. Had he rubbed my leg? That thought sent my creep-o-meter into the red zone.

I whipped around, made a second of eye contact, then slid into the booth across from Daisy. "Don't look behind you, but I think that guy touched my leg."

"Then maybe you should say hello." She held up her phone.

"He's facing this way. If you are trying to use your camera to see him, he'll know." I glanced over her shoulder, and his gaze dropped to the floor.

He'd been looking at me.

"Is he cute?" Daisy clearly wasn't taking me seriously.

I leaned halfway across the table. "Yes, very."

"Describe him."

"Seriously, Daisy? Don't you think touching me is a little bit creepy? Just a little?"

"I doubt he touched you. Want me to ask him?"

"No! I don't want you to ask him. I felt something brush the back of my leg. He's the only one that was anywhere close to me." I tried my best to keep my voice down, hoping he couldn't hear me.

"Tell me what he looks like."

I was practically laying on the table, so I was close enough to whisper. "He's got dark hair, dark brown eyes with little flecks of gold near the edges, and a little facial hair."

"Tall?"

"He's sitting down."

"You noticed the flecks in his eyes."

"He looked at me." I froze when I heard someone approach the table.

The mystery guy cleared his throat.

I slid back into my seat. After the day I'd had, I didn't want to make a scene at a restaurant fighting off a creep. I shifted, watching him out of the corner of my eye. I nonchalantly laid my hand on my fork. In an emergency, that utensil could be useful.

The good-looking, creepy stranger stared at the carpet and held out a folded napkin that matched the ones on our table. "You, um . . ." He rubbed his forehead. "You dropped this." He set the napkin in front of me, then hurried back to his table.

Those good shoulder lines continued all the way down. Why was I even looking? He was a total weirdo.

"Clearly he has problems because I didn't drop this

napkin." I picked it up to emphasize my point, and little sparkly princess panties landed on the table.

Daisy laughed. "He probably thinks you were *dropping hints* to him." She wasn't quiet or funny. "Get it? Dropping hints."

"I get it. Not funny."

The snicker behind her made it clear that the rather handsome man who had just dropped an undergarment on my table didn't agree with me.

The horror nauseated me and suffocated me at the same time. "He can't possibly think they're mine. Please. I couldn't get those on my thigh, let alone my . . ." I needed to shut up.

The man could hear every word.

Smiling, the waiter walked up, seemingly oblivious to the panties on the table. I grabbed them and shoved them into my purse.

"Have you decided?" He tapped his ordering pad.

Shaking my head, I tried to formulate words.

"Could we have a few more minutes?" Daisy saved the day.

"Sure. I'll be back in a bit." He checked in at the next table and received the same request.

I stared down at the table, my cheeks burning.

"Hey, you okay?" Daisy patted my hand. "Look at me."

"I'm sure I'll be fine . . . eventually. But when I look at you, I see him too because he's right behind you. He must think—"

"He probably thinks you're a young mom who is enjoying a night out."

"That might be worse than thinking I was coming onto him." I buried my head in my hands. "I have to explain. I can't sit here all through dinner, imagining what's running through his head. Because my imagination tells me he's thinking horrible things."

When I glanced up, the man made eye contact. His dark brown eyes invited me to talk to him. That was how it felt deep in my soul.

"If I die of embarrassment, please get rid of those panties before someone finds them in my purse." I squeezed Daisy's shoulder before walking to the next table. Crying now would only make things more awkward, but getting an up-close look at the man and seeing how good looking he was, I wanted to sob. If he was indeed single, I didn't want him thinking I was married.

Laugh lines crinkled near his mesmerizingly dark eyes. "Hi."

"I am so sorry about that."

He shook his head. "You don't—"

"But I do. I accused you, and I'm sorry." Fingers twisted into a knot, I pressed my thumbnail into the palm of my hand. "Even though you are a total stranger, I need you to know that those aren't mine. I babysat my niece and nephew, and she threw her clothes into the washer with mine. I couldn't find the dryer sheets, so everything clung together because of the static. Her . . . *clothes* must have stuck to the inside of my dress." I caught my breath after vomiting the explanation. "You believe me, don't you?"

He nodded. "I wasn't sure how to make it not awkward."

"The napkin was quick thinking." I ran a finger along the edge of the table. "Well, I should . . ." No part of me wanted to walk away which made no sense at all.

"Your niece must be in that sparkly stage. Three or four?"

I could've been less obvious about checking out his left hand. No ring. No suntan line either. Either he was a dad—whether he was sneaking around without a ring or divorced was a separate question—or an uncle with nieces, or something else entirely.

He furrowed his brow. "Oh, gosh. That probably

sounded—"

I put up a hand to silence him. "You're either sneaking out on your wife, an uncle, or seriously creepy. But I'm ruling out creepy because in that case, I think you would've kept them instead of embarrassing me."

He pointed to his left hand. "No wife. No kids. But I have three nieces. They are three, five, and seven. And I'm sorry I embarrassed you. I might've kicked them under the table and acted like it never happened, but I overheard what you said to your friend about something brushing the back of your leg."

I shrugged. "That's okay." Still standing next to his table, I wanted to melt into the carpet during the half second of awkward silence. "I should . . ." Why did I keep saying that?

He pointed at the other side of his booth. "You're welcome to join me. You and your friend."

"Um, thank you, but—"

"We'd love to join you." Daisy nudged me out of her way, then slid onto the bench. "I'll slide in first so that you two can continue your conversation. I'm Daisy." She'd sprung into action rather quickly.

I eased down onto the bench next to her, unsure whether to hug her or hit her.

"Nice to meet you, Daisy. I'm Javi." He smiled and turned his gaze back to me.

Usually, Daisy was the center of attention, but this guy focused on me. Flattering didn't begin to describe how it felt. No one would believe this story if I ever scraped together the nerve to tell it at any point in the future. "Short for Javier?"

"Yes." He rubbed his whiskers.

"I'm Bella. It's not short for anything." I stuck out my hand. "It's nice to meet you, Javi."

His strong warm fingers wrapped around mine. "The pleasure is all mine."

CHAPTER 2

JAVI

After a full day of meetings, I'd headed to the restaurant, seeking dinner and a quiet refuge. Normally, I worked from home. But booking new jobs meant meetings, so I'd driven up from San Antonio to Austin to meet with potential clients.

The brunette sitting across from me changed my entire plan for the evening. Flirting wasn't one of my talents, but staring at her without talking would be creepy, and I'd already toed that line.

When she and her friend joined me at the table, it felt almost like Christmas.

"I can't imagine keeping my nieces overnight. You must be a super aunt. Do they give out awards for that?" I wasn't in the habit of asking out complete strangers, but two seconds after Bella approached my table, I knew I wanted to see her again.

"They should give out awards." She laughed.

The sound was like watching sparks dance above a fire.

She lined up her silverware. "This was the first time I've

stayed with them for more than a few hours. And probably the last. My nephew isn't even one yet."

"That kept you busy, I'm sure."

"Yes. But the whole time I was taking care of him, my niece was talking. The. Whole. Time." Bella sighed and slumped back into her bench. "I need to quit talking. I haven't even looked at the menu."

Daisy brushed her red hair over her shoulder, then laid her menu on the table. "What do you do, Javi?"

If I had a wingman like her, I might not still be single at thirty-two. "I'm a freelance programmer."

Bella grinned but didn't look up. "Is that code for I work alone in a dark room?"

"Not a good code apparently." I pushed my menu to the side. "What do y'all do?"

Her eyes full of sparkle, she pointed at her friend. "Daisy is an *influencer*. She blogs about all things Texas."

What was I thinking inviting these ladies to sit with me? Hanging out with influencers was not my speed. "That sounds exciting."

Daisy shook her head. "It pays the bills, and I sort of love it. But Bella makes it sound way more glamorous than it is."

"That's what friends are for." Bella closed her menu. "She's in town this weekend to spend time with me and to take pictures of the Texas Capitol building. It's taller than the one in Washington. Did you know that?"

"I've heard that. Sounds like you have a fun weekend planned."

Daisy crossed her arms. "I'm leaving tomorrow afternoon. I had to make this a short trip."

"Where are you from?" I wanted to learn more about Bella, but too much was at stake to risk being perceived as rude. So I asked them both questions.

"San Antonio."

"Oh. Not too far." I decided to keep quiet about also residing in that fine city. That was information I could share if Bella and I went out on a date. "Bella, what about you? What do you do?" I loved the way her cheeks colored slightly when I said her name.

She pulled her dark hair over her shoulder. "I work at a bank, and I use my vacation time to babysit my sister's kids. That, in a nutshell, tells you how exciting my life is."

The waiter scratched his head as he walked up to the table. Focused on Bella, he chuckled. "Was there something wrong with that table?"

"Not really." She opened her menu and hid her face. "But I like this one better."

I bumped her foot under the table, and she grinned.

Now it really felt like Christmas. All I needed now was her number.

The waiter set desserts on the table. "Enjoy those slices of chocolate cake. They are decadent." He refilled the coffee mugs before walking away.

"Excuse me a second, ladies." I followed the waiter, and when we were out of earshot of my table, I handed him my credit card. "I want to pay the entire bill."

He squinted one eye. "How did you manage that? That redhead is stunning, and the brunette is far from ugly. And no offense, but you look like a college dropout who got spiffed up for an interview."

"None taken. It's just my lucky day. And it's the brunette who caught my eye." I probably needed to invest in new clothes. Or maybe having them cleaned and pressed would help.

He moved my card back and forth. "Congrats on your lucky day. I'll take care of this."

When I dropped back into my seat, Bella nudged my foot. "Thanks. You didn't have to pay for dinner."

How did she know?

Daisy moaned after popping a bite of chocolate cake in her mouth. "This is divine. And we totally saw you handing the waiter the card. We just couldn't figure out what he said to you."

My dignity stopped me from sharing that part of the story, but I brushed at the wrinkles in my shirt. "I've enjoyed tonight. Thank you for keeping me company." If I didn't ask now, I risked missing the opportunity to see Bella again. "Bella, would you be interested—"

"Yes. Even if you were about to say geocaching—is that even still a thing?" Her brown eyes sparkled with expectation.

The words that came tumbling out of her mouth intrigued me. Her lips alone intrigued me. How would they taste? Were they as soft as they looked?

"I wasn't thinking of geocaching, but I'd happily adjust my plans if that's what you'd like to do. Here's my number. Text me, and we can figure something out."

She shook her head and pursed her lips. "No."

Had I totally misheard what she'd said before? Had she changed her mind already? The waiter had my credit card, so slinking out of the restaurant wasn't an option. "Okay, well." I slid my business card back toward my side of the table.

Grabbing my hand, she sighed. "Sorry, I wasn't saying no to going out with you. I just—I want your number. Seriously, I really want that. But I don't want the pressure of texting you. I'll stare at the phone for an hour, trying to decide what message to send. No matter how long I think about it, the message will be boring and stupid. Too much pressure."

Laughing, I slid my phone across the table to her. "If you'll kindly add your number to my contacts, I will stare at my phone for an hour before sending you a boring message."

"Deal." She tapped on the screen, then handed back my phone. "I've had fun. Hanging out with you is way better than babysitting a seven-month-old."

"Thanks . . . I guess."

Guessing her age was difficult because the mix of hesitation and vivaciousness gave her a youthful air.

Daisy nudged Bella. "Let me out please. I'm going to visit the ladies' room before we leave."

Bella jumped up, then dropped back onto the seat. "I'm glad you didn't think I was a crazy person who was being ridiculous and trying to get your attention. And I am sorry I accused you. But when it fell, I felt it, and I thought you'd brushed my leg as I passed you."

"That's why you looked at me like that?"

Her head bobbed up and down. "But I know you didn't. You can see how I would think that, given the circumstances, right?"

"Are you always so entertaining?"

"I don't mean to be."

"Are you free on Sunday?" Driving from San Antonio to Austin on a Sunday meant traffic, but sitting bumper to bumper was worth it if she said yes.

A wide smile raised her cheek bones. "I am."

"Great. I'll text you tomorrow, and we'll figure out a plan."

Outside of work, I rarely took risks. Inviting two women to share my table and asking one out was so far from typical, I'd surprised myself.

While Bella stood to let Daisy back in, I typed out a quick text: *My evening turned out much better than expected thanks to static and sparkles.*

She sat down and glanced at her phone. Soft pink flooded her cheeks, and her brown eyes snapped up to meet my gaze.

Never before had I met someone who made my timid side sit quietly and fueled the risk taker buried deep inside me. Her reactions didn't make me feel like a bumbling fool.

I definitely wanted to see her again.

CHAPTER 3

BELLA

All the casual dresses I owned were strewn on my bed. I pulled on capri pants and a floral top. And I double-checked both pant legs to make sure no other clothing accompanied me out of the bedroom.

I checked the time. Javi should've been here already.

Pacing, I called Daisy. "He's seven minutes late. Tell me he hasn't changed his mind."

"He hasn't."

"Now tell me I shouldn't change *my* mind."

"You shouldn't. And if you do, I'm coming over there to scold you. He's a nice guy."

"He is, but I don't know him at all."

"That's why you're going out with him. To get to know him better. That's how this dating thing works . . . or so I'm told."

"Want me to see if he has a friend?"

"Maybe down the road. Go enjoy your date. But call me after. No matter what time."

"I will. He's here. Gotta go." I ended the call and opened the door.

Javi held out a bouquet of zinnias. "Thanks for not making me wait a whole week to see you again."

I clasped the bouquet and inhaled. "It was purely selfish on my part. Although I'm a bit surprised."

"Why is that?"

"Usually when Daisy and I go out somewhere . . . this isn't what happens."

His brow pinched. "I hope I didn't make her feel left out or excluded. I just wanted . . ." He shrugged. "To go out with *you*."

"That's what never happens. Guys don't want to go out with me. They ask her out all the time. She's the queen of first dates. But if the date is boring, she doesn't go on a second one. She rarely goes on second dates."

Javi stepped closer. "Those other guys must be out of their minds. You're captivating and funny."

I filled a glass with water and set the flowers in it. "Keep talking like that, and my cheeks are going to stay red all day."

"Promise? The color looks good on you." He held out his hand.

I trusted my fingers to his much bigger hand. "Lead the way."

He pointed at a GMC pickup. "That's mine. The blue one." After helping me in, he ran around to the driver's side. "I wanted to apologize for making you wait. The traffic getting up here was nuttier than I expected."

"Austin traffic can be bad. Where did you drive from?"

Driving, he kept his focus on the road. "San Antonio."

"You drove all the way up here to see me?"

"Totally worth it. Friday, I was in town on business. After dinner, I drove back home."

Surprised, I snapped my mouth shut before I repeated the question again. But when I opened my yapper what tumbled out wasn't much better. "You sure don't act like a guy who lives in his parents' basement and works on computers."

"No basement. My parents live in San Antonio, but in a different part of town."

"Where do you live?" I wanted to know everything I could about this guy who would drive two hours to see me.

His brow wrinkled. "In San Antonio." The words came out slowly, confusion evident.

"I know that. I mean . . . do you live alone in an apartment or in a high-rise condo or . . ." I shrugged.

"I own a house."

I shifted the seatbelt and turned to face him. "Do you live alone?"

"I have a housemate. He's a fireman, so he's only around a few days a week."

A mental note to introduce Daisy to the fireman got filed away in my brain.

"As you just saw, I have an apartment. I don't have a roommate anymore. I've married off three. I was kinda getting tired of that and of being a bridesmaid, but don't repeat that last part. I'm happy for them, but . . ."

"No need to explain." He chuckled. "I understand."

We parked outside the Wildflower Center.

"I thought we'd walk around here for a bit, then grab some lunch." He clasped my hand as we walked toward the entrance. "And I have a small surprise."

"Oh?" I could get used to being pampered and surprised.

He stuck his free hand in his pocket, then opened it after pulling it back out. In his palm lay an assortment of small trinkets: a six-sided die, a miniature pink flamingo, a happy face pin, and a Strawberry Shortcake eraser. "I brought stuff to put in the geocaching boxes."

"You aren't serious!"

"You weren't *dropping hints* that you secretly wanted to hunt for hidden treasure?"

I snaked my arms around his waist and hugged him. "You are so fun."

His breath caught.

"Sorry, I sort of sprang that hug on you. I should've asked."

He leaned down to make eye contact because I was staring at the buttons on his shirt. "That was a happy surprise. Completely happy."

I gave him another squeeze. "Good to know."

After paying the entrance fee, he opened an app, and we hunted for the caches. Laughing our way down the garden paths and through the wildflower meadow, we found the treasure boxes, signed the logbooks, and traded our goodies for others.

Two hours later, we climbed back into his truck.

"In the seven years since I graduated from college, this is, hands down, the best date I've ever been on." I clicked my seatbelt into place, glad we were going to eat because I wasn't ready for the date to be over.

He squinted and tapped his chin. "So you're saying that in college, you had a date that was more fun."

"That's not what I meant. How's this? In all my twenty-five years, I've never had more fun on a date."

He pulled my hand to his lips. "I'm really happy to hear that."

After talking for two hours at lunch, we drove to the Arboretum to get ice cream. He ordered chocolate, which seemed like a perfect complement to my peanut butter ice cream.

We sat on the cow sculptures and continued talking.

"Any other siblings besides your sister?" He leaned against the marble cow I was using as my perch.

"Only an older sister. And no matter how it sounded on Friday night, I do love her kids. What about you?"

"I'm sure I'd love them if I met them, but . . ." He shrugged and stepped away, anticipating my attempted swat. "I have one brother and one sister. He's older. She's younger. He's married and has three girls. She's also married and is expecting."

We tossed questions back and forth. Long after our ice cream was gone, we were engrossed in conversation.

I glanced at my phone when it buzzed. "Oh my gosh. It's almost seven." I let Daisy's call roll to voicemail.

A text from her popped up a second later. *Should I call the police?*

"You might want to respond to that one." Javi pointed toward a bench. "I'll be over—"

I caught his arm. "Please don't leave. You can hear whatever I tell her." I hit her number at the top of my favorites. "Daisy, hi. Sorry I missed your call. I was talking with Javi."

"Still? I thought he picked you up at ten this morning."

"He did. It's been an awesome date. We went geocaching." I pulled the phone away from my ear because her laughter caused pain to my eardrums.

"Call me when you get home. Seriously." She hung up.

I slid off the cow and laced my fingers with his. "This has been an awesome date."

"Maybe next weekend, if you're free, we'll drive out to the Hill Country and pick strawberries. And in June, we can pick blackberries or blueberries. July is supposed to be the best time for peaches."

My heart kicked into overdrive just thinking about

spending weekends with Javi. "I love your plan for the summer."

"Wonderful." He tugged me closer. "I've enjoyed today."

"Me too." I tilted my head back ever so slightly. Now, I was dropping hints.

Would he notice?

As he leaned closer, I closed my eyes. Something or someone tapped my leg. I opened one eye and looked down.

A little girl not much older than my niece pointed at the cow. "Can I sit up there?"

She seriously interrupted a first kiss because of a cow?

Javi laughed. "We'll get out of your way." He tucked an arm around my waist. "My goal is to make our next date more awesome than this one."

"That's a big goal. We've spent nine hours together, and I'm not even tired of you."

We stopped beside his truck.

"In that case, will you have dinner with me?"

"Tonight? Really? You have so far to drive."

"Traffic is crazy right now. Leaving later will be easier."

I pressed a hand to his chest, then slid my fingers up to his neck. "Before we go, let's pick up where we were interrupted."

His strong arms wrapped around me, and he brushed his lips on mine. He tasted a little like chocolate.

I didn't want to get ahead of myself, but the man was perfect.

CHAPTER 4

JAVI

My arms loaded with peaches, I pushed open my front door. "Hey, Adam. I'm glad you're here. I wanted to ask you about something."

Adam followed me into the kitchen, questions etched on his face. "First, what's with all the peaches?"

"It's July. Peach season. Bella and I picked them this weekend. I'm going to take them to my mom's I'm hoping I can get a peach cobbler out of the deal."

He rubbed his hands together. "Can't wait to taste it. I'm guessing things are going well with Bella. You've been out of town every weekend since the middle of May."

Things were going well. I worked extra on weeknights to be able to leave before traffic snarled. That made it possible to have dinner with Bella on Friday nights.

"I'm not complaining. Not a bit." I washed two peaches before tossing him one. "Bella has a friend. She's cute. Super nice. I thought maybe . . ." I let the offer dangle, hoping he'd jump on the idea.

But no. He shook his head. "Sorry. I'm not in the market for blind dates currently. I met someone. We went out last weekend, and we've seen each other a few times since. She's great."

"Why haven't I heard about this?" I grabbed a napkin as peach juice trailed down my chin.

Adam laughed, then snagged a napkin for himself. "Maybe because we've hardly seen each other the last few weeks. Between my shift schedule and your trips to Austin, there hasn't been a chance to catch you up."

I pulled a Coke out of the fridge. "Tell me about your new squeeze."

"I like her a lot, but she's not crazy about dogs. We'll have to see how that plays out." He crossed his fingers. "When are you going to propose? You can tell me to move out. I'd understand."

Although that thought had bounced around in my head, it sounded odd hearing the words out loud. Wasn't it too soon for talk about rings and marriage? Logic said one thing. My heart said another. "It's a bit too soon for a ring yet, but I'll let you know if you need to move out. Clearly, I'm crazy about her. I drive in Austin traffic every weekend just to see her."

"Totally crazy." Adam threw the peach pit in the trash. "But the best kind."

I glanced at the time. "I'm going to put these where the dogs can't get at them, and I'll take them to Mom tomorrow. Have a good night."

"You're going to go call her, aren't you?" Adam slipped his phone out of his pocket.

"Yep." I grabbed my phone and called Bella.

She answered on the first ring. "You made it?"

"I'm home." I sat on my bed and kicked my shoes off. "Have you made anything with your peaches?"

"I've eaten way too many. They are so good. I prepped

some to make a cobbler for Friday night. Do you like peach cobbler?"

"I do. Almost as much as I like you."

"Then maybe I should make two."

"I can't wait." I stifled a yawn, hoping she didn't notice.

She sighed. "I feel bad that you drive so far every weekend."

"It's not so bad."

"I just wish we lived closer, you know?"

I wished that every day. "If I didn't own a house, I might be looking for an apartment up there."

"Please don't think I was suggesting you need to move. I miss you is all."

Flopped back on the bed, I chose my words carefully. "I think about you all the time. Even when I'm working, there is a tiny neon sign blinking your name in the corner of my brain. I'd drive to Oklahoma or New Mexico every weekend to see you if that's what it took."

"Oh, Javi."

"But don't worry. I didn't think you were *dropping hints*."

"I'm never going to live that down, am I?"

I laughed. "I have to give static its due."

She inhaled, which signaled that a question was coming.

I waited.

"My parents asked about you. Would you . . . maybe . . ."

After we'd seen each other every weekend for two months, meeting her parents seemed the right thing to do. "I'd love to meet them."

"Great. They'll be excited. We'll probably all go to Martha's house, so you'll get to meet everyone."

"That will give me a chance to thank Natalie for washing her clothes with yours."

"They have no idea how we met. I'd like to keep it that way."

"All right then." I pulled the phone away as I yawned again.

"You need to sleep. I'm going to let you go."

"Before we hang up, go open that book on your coffee table." I'd taken a leap and made plans for months down the road, but I had no doubt I'd still be interested.

"The Texas Hill Country book with all the photographs?" Shuffling sounded as she crawled out of bed. "Where in the book?"

"I used a business card to mark the page." I waited for her to find it.

Pages flipped, and I held my breath.

"Johnson City? Why did you mark that page?"

"I thought maybe we'd visit there between Christmas and New Year's. Their Lights Spectacular is . . . well, spectacular."

Her soft gasp made me think she liked the idea. "I'd love that."

"Good. I'll book us rooms. I'm hoping . . . if my week goes well, I'll get into Austin early enough to meet you for lunch on Friday."

She blew a kiss into the phone. "Goodnight."

BELLA INHALED as I pulled up to the curb in front of a house draped in twinkling Christmas lights.

She exhaled slowly. "I probably should've mentioned that my sister has this weird fascination with Christmas in July. Well, with Christmas in general. But she celebrates it twice a year."

Biting back a laugh, I reached for Bella's hand. "Are we talking tree and everything?"

She nodded. They have an artificial tree for summer. They get a real tree the first week of November.

"Before Thanksgiving?" I'd grown up with the tradition of decorating the tree the day after Thanksgiving.

Her brow furrowed. "It might be best if you don't ask that question inside. Please."

The worry in her eyes would've amused me if it didn't break my heart.

"I promise not to start an incident. Please tell me you aren't concerned that a few Christmas lights will change the way I feel about you. It's your sparkly personality that has me captivated."

She turned a deep shade of red. "And whatever you do, do not mention how we met."

I pulled her in for a quick kiss before we climbed out of the car.

Christmas music greeted us when she pushed open the front door. "We're here." She tightened her grip on my hand as her family swarmed toward the front door.

Only four people raced to the door, but it felt like a swarm.

"Javi, this is my mom, Nancy, and my dad, Paul. And this is Martha and Owen." Bella pointed as she introduced each person.

I shook hands with each of them, desperately trying to store the names in my memory bank. When someone tugged on my pant leg, I let go of Bella's hand and squatted in front of Natalie. "Hi."

She grinned, then cocked her head. "Do you roar?"

While the truth lay somewhere between yes and no, having more context for the question seemed a necessity before answering. "Do you mean like a lion?"

She shrugged. "Any sort of beast."

The word beast was mildly disturbing until I remembered my princess trivia. "You mean like the sort of beast who has a flower with petals falling off?"

Her eyes brightened. "Bella loves the beast."

"In that case, I'll learn to roar."

She held out a candy cane. "Want one? Mommy hangs them on the tree but only up high where Nathan can't reach. I'm tall enough though."

"Maybe in a little while." In truth, I wasn't sure if she'd already licked on the one she offered me. Pulling a candy cane off the tree myself was a better option.

Talking to Natalie, I'd mostly ignored the audience. So, when Bella threw her arms around me, it caught me off guard. Suddenly conscious of everyone watching, I didn't hold her as long as I would've liked.

She kissed my cheek. "Natalie's right, you know."

"About me being a beast?" Heat pricked my skin, and I wondered if Martha had a fire blazing in her living room.

Owen took pity on me. "No reason for us all to stand around by the front door. Come on in. We have sherbet punch and bottled water in the kitchen."

"And food will be ready in about three minutes." Martha clapped her hands.

Nathan voiced his frustration with being left alone in the living room, and I prided myself on the fact that I knew the kids' names without Bella introducing them today.

We all walked into the kitchen, and I served myself a glass of the green sherbet punch, avoiding the cranberries floating on the top. I couldn't begin to imagine what Martha's house looked like when it was really Christmas.

With Nathan on her hip, Martha motioned for people to sit down at the table. "I don't think Bella has mentioned how y'all met. You live in San Antonio, isn't that right, Javi?"

Without dropping my punch, I pulled Bella into a hug which drew sappy sighs from her mom and sister. But I did it so they wouldn't see the blush I knew was creeping up Bella's cheeks. "She captured my attention when I was having dinner here in town. She and her friend Daisy were sitting in the next booth." I dropped a quick kiss on the top of Bella's head. "I invited them to sit with me, and Bella and I hit it off. I've been memorizing every inch of pavement between San Antonio and Austin most weekends since then."

Grinning, she looked up at me, then spun around to face her family. "Isn't he just the most romantic man you've ever met?"

So far, I was surviving Christmas in July quite well. I could only hope that our actual Christmas was just as merry.

CHAPTER 5

BELLA

"Thanks for covering for me." I climbed into the truck. "The question completely caught me off guard."

"Happy to help." Javi pulled away from the curb.

"You aren't driving back tonight, are you?"

He'd been pretty quiet about where he was staying.

"Oh, no. I'm just going to get a room in a hotel close to here. You're stuck with me tomorrow too." His wonderful grin warmed me to my toes.

I didn't even want to think about how much he'd spent doing that over the last few months. "Javi, you are welcome to my couch. I mean, I get it if you want something more comfortable. But if the only reason you are staying somewhere else is . . ." I wasn't sure how to word it. "I'm just letting you know I wouldn't feel weird about you crashing on my couch." I wanted to spend every minute possible with him, and having him leave at the end of the night was almost as bad as watching him leave at the end of the weekend.

"If you don't mind, I'll do that." He opened his hand on the center console which attracted my hand like a magnet. "I enjoyed meeting your family. They didn't chase me out of the house with a bat, so that's good."

"Of course they didn't. You're amazing." When he squeezed my hand, I blew him a kiss. "Just perfect."

When we arrived at the apartment, he carried his bag up. "Let's sit for a second."

The seriousness in his tone had me worried. Was my family too eccentric for his taste? What if he asked for things to cool off after I'd already invited him to stay over? That would be uncomfortable.

Preparing myself for whatever, I clasped my hands together in my lap. "What's up?"

"I'm crazy about you." The man had a talent for opening lines. He'd just guaranteed that I'd be hanging on his every word. "That's probably pretty obvious by the fact that I show up almost every weekend. But I wanted you to hear me say it."

I nodded, grinning at him.

"But..."

That was truly an awful word. "But what?"

Laugh lines crinkled near his eyes, and he reached for my hand. "But because there is a significant age difference—"

"Seven years isn't that big a gap. I've known people who were born ten years apart. One friend even married a guy fifteen years older."

"If I thought it was too big a gap, I wouldn't have asked you out. And we also live in different cities. I'm trying to say that I'd like to take it slow."

"Is this because I said you could sleep in my apartment?"

"Partially. And after meeting your parents, I wanted you to know where I stood—relationship wise. I've booked us rooms the week between Christmas and New Year's. I'm not seeing anyone else and don't plan to. Anything else I need to add?"

I shifted and draped my legs over his lap. "So, just to be sure I understood, let me recap. You like me. A lot. And you are willing to drive up every weekend for an indefinite amount of time until we decide to have another conversation like this."

He slipped his arms around me. "You summed it up well and made my little speech sound completely unnecessary."

"It was sweet. You want to give me time to see all your flaws." The word 'before' almost slipped out, but I caught it in time. And that was good because there was no taking-it-slow way of finishing that phrase.

"Exactly. I want you to have plenty of time before . . ." He'd made the slip I'd managed to avoid. "Before we have this conversation again." Smooth. The man was smooth.

Rewarding him for his quick thinking, I pressed a kiss to his lips. "And just so you can hear me say it, I like you too."

He chuckled. "Thanks. I had fun tonight."

"I'm glad Martha's fondness for Christmas didn't scare you away."

"How long has she been so festive?"

"I'll answer in just a sec. I'm going to change, then make us tea or hot cocoa or something." I ran toward my room. "I might even have a bottle of wine if you want that."

While I pulled clothes out of my drawer, I texted Daisy with one hand. *He met my family. And he didn't even seem to mind celebrating Christmas when walking outside makes you sweat.*

She replied right away, almost as if she'd been waiting to hear from me. *Yay! Any other news?* A smile face with hearts for eyes followed her text.

I tossed the phone on the bed as I yanked on leggings. After slipping on a shirt, I answered: *He's sleeping on my couch tonight.*

Have fun! Daisy was my best friend, and having her in my corner meant the world to me.

When I walked back into the living room, Javi leaned out of the kitchen. His dress shirt was missing, replaced with a well-worn t-shirt. And he'd traded his khakis for jeans. "I found the wine. Would you like a glass?"

"Please."

I snuggled into one end of the sofa.

After handing me a glass, he sat down next to me, then draped my legs across his lap. He sipped the wine and smiled. "This is good."

"The wine? Or being snuggled on the couch?"

"Both."

"Back to Martha's fascination with Christmas in July. Her first year of high school, she befriended a girl who'd just moved from North Carolina. That girl had gone to a summer camp where they celebrated Christmas in July every summer. They'd have a big party. Santa even showed up."

"He must've been roasting in that suit in summer."

"Probably. Anyway, that camp is credited for starting the Christmas in July party idea back in the thirties. We have them to thank." I could get used to being snuggled on the couch with Javi. "Martha already loved Christmas. That just gave her a way to love it even more."

Javi shook his head. "Owen must have quite a story to tell."

I wasn't quite ready to tell Javi that story or about the Christmas-themed wedding in July. Easing him into my family slowly gave our relationship a better chance of success.

CHAPTER 6

JAVI

I paced through the house, trying to decide what to do. My mom had been talking about Thanksgiving since Easter. Having all her kids at the table fed her soul. As much as I wanted to make her happy, the idea of being away from Bella at Thanksgiving left me unsettled.

Dialing her number, I flopped back on the bed. "Hi there. How was your day?"

She sighed. "People are grumpy. They are too busy thinking about what to serve at Thanksgiving to smile or be nice."

"I'm sorry. Maybe if you wear a Santa hat, it'll put people in a better mood. I bet Martha has one you could borrow."

"I'm not quite that desperate yet." Her soft laugh made me want to reach through the phone.

"I've been thinking about Thanksgiving. We didn't really talk about it this past weekend." And that was my fault for not bringing it up. "My mom is very excited about having all of us at home. My married siblings alternate between families, and this is the year they are with my side. I'd love for you to join me."

She made a noise that sounded like a sniffle which wasn't at all the response I'd expected.

I dragged my fingers through my hair. "What's wrong?"

"I don't feel like I can. It's Martha's year with Owen's family. His parents live out of state." She sighed. "I'd love to spend the day with you, but that would leave Mom and Dad alone. What about the day after Thanksgiving? Are you free then?"

"Just tell me when and where you want me to meet you the day after Thanksgiving." I had no problem skipping the tree decorating.

Watching kids hang ornaments was far more entertaining for my parents than watching me hang ornaments.

"Great! I'm not even sure what we'll do, but I'm glad I'll get to see you."

"You're one of the things I'm most thankful for this year." I skated perilously close to words I wanted to say in person.

I loved this woman, and I couldn't wait to see her face when I told her.

WITH TWO OF my nieces in my lap and the other hanging over the back of my chair, I fumbled my phone as I tried to answer. "Hello."

"Hi! The turkey will be out of the oven in just a bit, so I thought I'd sneak in a phone call before I have to eat. What about you?"

"I'm on sitter duty. The ladies are in the kitchen prepping food, and my dad and the other guys are outside deep frying the turkey."

My oldest niece tapped my arm. "Is that your girlfriend?"

When had anyone around her been talking about my girlfriend?

I nodded.

"Sounds like you have your hands full." Bella sounded wistful.

"For sure. Soon, we'll have to get you down here to San Antonio, so you can meet everyone."

"I'd love that."

The tapping started again. "Can I talk to her?" My niece grinned as if that would convince me.

I was probably going to regret my choice. "Bella, my niece would like to talk to you. Is that okay?"

"Absolutely."

Kayla grabbed the phone. "Hi. Are you coming over to have turkey?"

Leaning in close, I strained to hear. Kayla walked away from my chair, shooting me a look that indicated she found my eavesdropping rude.

She sat in a chair across the room. "My name is Kayla. Maybe you can come for Christmas."

I really didn't need her help arranging a time for Bella to meet my family. "That's long enough. Let me have the phone."

The five-year-old, Emily, jumped off my lap. "My turn." After a brief struggle, she walked away with the phone. "My name is Emily. I'm five."

With Rachel on my hip, I chased after Emily, eager to have my phone back. And when I retrieved it, I handed it to the little one. "Just say a quick hello."

Grinning, Rachel touch the screen and put the phone on speaker. "Hi. Uncle Javi said I could talk to you."

Bella laughed. "Does he know you have his phone?" She'd caught on to what was happening on my end of the line.

"Yes. He's right here. Bella is a pretty name."

"Thank you. What's your name?"

"Rachel. I'm three." She wriggled out of my arms. "Bye."

I took the phone off speaker. "I should have given that choice more thought. Sorry about that."

"It was fun talking to them. I'd love to see you playing uncle. Hang on." She mumbled something I couldn't understand. Maybe her hand was covering the phone. "I need to go. Food is almost ready. Call me later."

"I will."

The call ended. I couldn't wait until tomorrow. It was definitely time for another conversation.

CHAPTER 7

BELLA

My arms loaded with bags, I fumbled with my keys. Javi would be here soon. I dropped the bags onto the couch and pulled out the assorted ornaments and twinkle lights I'd purchased. Putting up a tree had never been a priority for me in years past.

Mom and Dad had one up every year, and, well, Martha spread enough Christmas cheer for multiple people. I wasn't a Scrooge, but I didn't go overboard... until this year.

Thinking of Javi's comment about decorating the day after Thanksgiving, I'd shopped my little heart out. The colorful array of decorations made me happy. Instead of choosing a color scheme, I'd gone the kid-in-a-candy-store route. Anything that caught my eye went into the cart. There was a slight possibility I'd bought more than a tree would hold.

I tossed the bags in the recycling bin, shoved everything to one side of the sofa so that Javi would have a place to sit, and grabbed my phone when it rang. "Hi there."

"Hello, my beautiful Bella. I should be there in just a few minutes unless something goes horribly wrong with traffic."

"When you say things like that, you invite trouble. You know that, right?"

He laughed. "You're probably correct. I can't wait to see you."

"Me too." I almost suggested that I meet him in the lot so we could run to get a tree, but I wanted a chance to say hello. And by that I meant kissing him without leaning across a car to do it. "Did you enjoy Thanksgiving with your family?"

"I did. But I missed you."

Spending Thanksgiving without him had exploded a truth in my heart which had previously flickered in a corner: I loved him and didn't want to spend anymore holidays without him. After our Christmas in July family gathering, when he'd explained that because of the age difference—was seven years that big a deal? Anyway, because of that, we were taking things slowly . . . especially since we'd dated long distance the entire time. But I was tired of slow.

Lost in thought, I yelped when a knock sounded.

Javi laughed from outside. "I even warned you and still managed to surprise you."

I threw open the door. "I was deep in thought."

"About?" He slid his arms around my waist and pulled me close.

I hovered my lips close to his. "You."

We enjoyed several minutes of saying hello.

Kissing me, Javi kicked the door closed, then walked me toward the couch. He pulled me into his lap as he sat down. When we came up for air, he glanced around. "Has Martha been here?"

I swatted his chest. "No. I shopped. I thought maybe we could go get a tree and decorate today."

"You remembered?"

"I did. Do you like the idea?"

"I love the idea." He patted my hip. "Let's go get a tree. We can pick up lunch while we're out."

"Perfect. Let me pull my shoes on." I hopped out of his lap.

When he stood and turned around, I slapped a hand over my mouth. "Oh no!" With only one shoe on, I raced over and swiped at his backside.

"Um . . . Bella?" He looked back over his shoulder. "What are you doing?"

I pointed at the glittery ornaments. "Those were all over the couch at first. I didn't realize they shed so much, but now your backside is all . . ."

"Sparkly?"

I nodded.

He picked up my other shoe. "I'll look extra festive. And I'll shake my booty on the tree lot to knock a bit off."

"That I want to see!" I hooked my purse on my shoulder. "I'm ready."

He stared at me, smiling. "I think I am too."

"Wait! I got us something to wear to the tree lot." I yanked two Santa hats out of the pile of décor. "Festive, huh?"

"And it matches the glitter." He put the hat on the top of his head. "Suddenly, I feel jolly."

Holding hands, we walked out to his truck. He opened my door and gave me a quick kiss before helping me in. "Does your family do a big Christmas Eve celebration or is Christmas morning the big focus?"

Heart racing, I squeezed his hand. "Christmas morning . . . pajamas and all."

"Matching?" He lifted an eyebrow.

"No. Absolutely not. There are limits." I buckled in as he ran around to the driver's seat.

"I'm surprised Martha doesn't insist on matching Christmas pajamas."

Bella laughed, filling my truck with that musical sound. "What about your family?"

"Christmas Eve we get together for tamales and gifts. Not all gifts are opened that night, but we each open at least one."

"What a fun tradition!"

"I know it would mean a lot of driving, but I'd love for you to join us that night." He reached for my hand. "If you'd like that."

"I'd *love* that. And maybe, you could be with my family on Christmas morning."

"I'll start shopping for pajamas." He winked.

After parking at the tree lot, he dusted off his seat. "There was more than a little glitter on me, wasn't there?"

"It was noticeable." I dusted off his pants.

He caught my hand. "That's enough of that. Let's go find the perfect tree."

We strolled past the super tall trees. They were stunning, but there was no way they'd fit inside my apartment.

"I forgot to get something for on top of the tree!"

"What goes on top? Angel or star or something else?" He spun a tree to look at the other side, then shook his head at a huge bare spot.

"Is that an opinion question or is there a right answer?" I didn't really have a preference.

Chuckling, he pulled out another tree. "Opinion. Our tree has had an angel for years and years but that's because it belonged to my grandparents—the angel, not the tree."

"Either is fine with me. I love the idea of having something special or sentimental."

"What about a tree stand?"

"I don't care if that's sentimental. Functional is more important." I bumped his shoulder.

"We can get one here." Grinning, he scooted a tree away

from the others. "What about this one? It's not too big, and the branches look good."

The tree had branches perfectly spaced. "It's great."

"Perfect. Let's buy this one." He nodded toward the cashier. "You want to get him while I hold the tree?"

"We can just carry it over there. Together." I reached for the top of the tree.

"Got it?" He lifted the other end.

I glanced back and grinned at his wide smile and Santa hat. "I haven't been this excited about Christmas since I was a kid."

"I feel the same way."

We made our way to the register and paid for the tree. Once it was securely in the truck, we headed back to my apartment.

Javi was quiet as we drove. After parking, he slapped his forehead. "I forgot to stop for food."

"We'll order pizza."

"That works. Good. If you'll get the tree stand, I'll grab the tree." He jumped out and swiped at the back of his jeans. He still sparkled as he walked.

As I passed the back window, I glanced into the backseat of the truck. A box wrapped in colorful paper and tied with a bright red bow sat on the floorboard. Now I was even more excited.

CHAPTER 8

JAVI

Catching Bella's expression when she spotted the present made me eager to get the decorating underway. When I'd bought the gift, I hadn't planned to be trimming the tree with her. But her plans for the day made it even more perfect.

After carrying in the tree, I ran back out to the truck and grabbed the present.

She eyed me as I walked back inside.

"Why don't you order the pizza while I get the tree situated in the stand. It may take me a few grumbles to get it straight."

Laughing, she picked up her phone.

I set to work. Stretched out on the floor, I adjusted the base. Then I stood to assess the straightness. The tree leaned to the left. Back down on the floor, I adjusted the base again. I let loose a few choice words, albeit quietly, because the tree now leaned to the right and forward.

I was getting more exercise getting up and down off the floor than I'd gotten all week . . . which said a lot about my exercise routine this week. Normally good about carving out time for that sort of thing, I'd been a complete lump during the Thanksgiving week.

Working on the base again, I inhaled before getting back up.

"Wait. A little more to the right. And back just a hair." Bella stood next to my legs. "Pizza will be here in a half hour."

I followed her instructions, adjusting until she said it was perfect. When I stood up, I sighed. "Finally. Should we put the lights in first or . . ."

"Or what?" Her face brightened.

Tugging her close, I whispered, "Or would you like to open the gift I brought?"

"That's what I want to do first. The curiosity is killing me."

I tweaked her nose. "I definitely don't want that."

She brushed at the couch cushion before sitting down and tearing the paper off the gift. As soon as she'd lifted the lid off the box, she gasped. "An angel!"

"For the top of your tree. There are lights inside that shine through the punched tin. And she's holding a heart so you'll be reminded that I love you." I dropped down next to her. "Because I do."

Tears slipped down her cheeks as she hugged it to her chest. "It's brand new, and it's already special. I love it." She cupped my cheek with one hand. "And I love you more than Martha loves Christmas."

Telling her how I felt had moved us one step closer to a discussion about marriage. But I wanted that conversation kicked off by a question. I had no doubts that I wanted to marry her. My doubts were all about where to live. Living in two different cities made it a tad more complicated.

"You look so pensive." She grazed her thumb along my cheek. "What's wrong?"

"Nothing's wrong. I just wish we lived in the same city."

She blinked, then pressed a soft kiss to my lips. "We'll figure it out. Seriously."

Threading my fingers into her hair, I silently promised her forever. The ring was coming, but right now, we both knew we were in love. It truly felt like Christmas.

"I should get the lights on the tree before the pizza arrives."

She turned on Christmas tunes, and I pulled the lights out of the boxes. I'd learned over the years not to trust a brand-new strand, or any strand. I plugged in the lights to make sure they all blinked.

Then, with me on one side of the tree and Bella on the other, we wrapped the tree in multiple strands of colorful twinkling lights.

Once the tree was all aglow, she picked up the angel. "Now this."

I plugged it into the end of the light strand. "Climb up onto the ladder. You should put it on top."

Clutching my hand, she climbed up onto the step ladder and set the angel on the top of the tree. As she stepped down into my arms, someone knocked.

The pizza guy had awful timing.

EATING pizza and watching the tree blink, Bella told me about their holiday traditions.

"It wasn't a surprise to any of us that Martha decided to get married in July. Poor Owen was a good sport about all of it . . . fake snow and all." She tossed her crust onto her plate. "My hair was so nasty from all the *snow*." She used finger quotes to emphasize the last word. "Snow and sundresses. That could've been her theme."

I pointed at her unfinished crusts. "Mind if I eat those?"

"Help yourself. They are too bready—that's not a word, but you know what I mean, right?"

"It means more food for me. So . . . I'm curious. Your parents' names and your sister's name are all . . ." I didn't know how to finish my question.

"Are you asking why they have names that were probably in the top one hundred in nineteen fifty and my name isn't?"

"That's exactly what I'm asking."

Her cheeks colored a deep rose. "For my parents tenth wedding anniversary, Martha stayed with my grandparents, and my parents spent a week in Italy. Is that enough of an explanation?" She met my gaze for only a split second. "Please say that's enough."

I kissed the side of her head. "I get it." I picked up the empty pizza box and the paper plates. "Now for the ornaments."

"What about your name?"

"I have no idea. I guess they just liked the sound of it. To be honest, I never asked." After shoving the trash into the can, I held out a hand to Bella. "Thank you for all of this . . . the ornaments and decorating the tree."

"Even the glitter?"

I wiggled my butt. "Even that."

With Christmas music blaring, we hung ornaments on the tree. And if the ring had been in my pocket, I might've proposed on the spot.

CHAPTER 9

BELLA

Snuggled beside Javi, I sipped my hot cocoa. "Did your family decorate today?"

He glanced at his watch. "They'll start that in about two hours. My brother had something going on this morning, so they were getting together this evening."

"We have time! If we leave now, you can be there to decorate with your family."

He blinked, his smile widening. "We? You'll come with me?"

"Yes. If you want me to."

"I want you to."

"Let me just throw a few things in a bag. I'll text Daisy and let her know I'm coming. I can crash at her place." Almost to my room, I stopped. "We don't have to do this. It's kind of spur of the moment, and maybe they don't like those kinds of surprises."

"I love the idea. And I can't wait for them to meet you. They'll love you too."

"I can take my own car if that makes it easier. That way you don't have to drive all the way back."

"Are you kidding? I want to spend two hours with you in a car . . . in traffic. More opportunity for you to see my flaws."

"I'm not sure there's anything you could say or do at this point that would change my mind." I leaned against the wall and crossed my arms.

We'd spent enough time together that I wasn't operating under the illusion that he was perfect, but we'd spent enough time together for me to know he was perfect for me.

He strolled across the room. "Is that so?"

"But I'm really looking forward to meeting your nieces. I bet they'll answer any question I throw at them."

Pulling me close, he laughed. "For sure. But if we don't hurry, we won't get to see them before they get grumpy. You pack a bag. I'll let them know were coming."

I kissed him before running into my room.

"Pack enough for the rest of the weekend. I'll entertain you until you need to be home." Javi knew how to make me feel loved.

After a quick glance at the forecast, I packed accordingly, then threw in two other outfits just in case the weather guys were wrong. What were the chances of that?

Twelve minutes later, we were on the road to San Antonio.

"What did they say?"

"Mom said not to speed because she needs time to clean the bathrooms and make dinner."

Horror gripped me. "She doesn't have to clean for me. I don't care if the bathroom is dirty."

Javi clasped my hand. "Don't worry about it. It just means she's really excited about you coming."

That last part thrilled me.

I shot off a text to Daisy: *On my way to San Antonio with*

Javi. We're going to meet with his family to decorate the tree. Mind if I sleep at your place?

You know I don't mind. You have a key! I can't wait to see you and get an update in person. So excited for you. Daisy was the best kind of friend.

"Your housemate, the fireman, is he still seeing someone? I only ask because I'm always scouting out eligible bachelors for Daisy."

"He sees her every chance he gets. I'm guessing he'll be engaged before the end of the year. Possibly."

"Oh." There went that grand plan. "I mean, I'm happy for him."

Javi winked. "I'll let you know if I meet someone worthy of Daisy."

"Thanks."

Time passed quickly as we talked and laughed. Before I knew it, he was parking along the curb in front of a one-story ranch-style home.

He leaned across the cab of the truck and kissed me. "I'm excited for you to meet everyone. But I think I said that already."

"No, before you said you were excited for them to meet me. That's different."

He ran around an opened my door. "I'm excited for both."

We didn't even make it to the front door before it swung open. Three little girls came running out. The two older ones ran right up in front of me. The littlest ran up to Javi and put her arms in the air.

He let go of my hand only long enough to pick her up. "This is Rachel. That's Kayla and Emily."

"Nice to meet you. I'm Bella." I had no doubt I was going to love being here.

When we made it to the porch, his mother smothered me

with a hug. "I have prayed for this day. Too much time on those computers had me worried he'd never find someone to love."

More talk like that, and I'd be a blubbering mess the rest of the night.

Mrs. Martinez hugged me again. "Come in."

An amazing aroma greeted me as I walked inside. "Whatever you made smells amazing."

She beamed. "It's a special day."

After a flurry of greetings and hugs, everyone settled at the table. It wasn't hard to see where Javi got his good looks from. Mr. Martinez had the same strong build and kind eyes.

I didn't feel like a stranger for long.

Hands down, my favorite part of the evening was watching Rachel seek out Javi's attention. She spent half the meal in his lap, tapping him on the arm any time she wanted to get his attention.

His poor shirt had greasy handprints all over it.

He caught me watching and winked at me. My heart threatened to burst. I loved him more than I knew how to say.

I leaned over and pressed a kiss to his cheek. "I'm glad we came."

At the end of the meal, Mrs. Martinez stood. "Leave the dishes on the table. We'll take care of them later. Everyone to the living room."

Javi tucked an arm around my waist. "Now for the fun part."

"This has all been fun. I like seeing you around your family." I sat next to him on the sofa.

Mr. Martinez lifted lids off several bins. "Rachel, you're first. Come pick out an ornament."

She beamed and took two minutes searching through the

boxes until she held up a princess in a yellow dress. Smiling, she hung it on the tree.

Javi draped an arm around me. "I don't think that was a coincidence."

"Are you my Beast?"

My answer was a soft gentle kiss.

The ornament hanging continued. After each of the girls chose one to hang, the ladies took their turns, then the men. After Mr. Martinez hung an ornament, the cycle ended. Everyone swarmed the bins.

"Now we all work together. We only take turns at the beginning." Javi kissed my cheek and pulled me toward the commotion.

Laughter filled the house as we tripped over each other covering the tree with colorful ornaments. When the green branches held more than their weight limit, Mrs. Martinez handed a treetop angel to Javi. "Will you put this up for me?"

He nestled it into place on the very top. "Merry Christmas!"

This was going to be the best Christmas ever.

I HUGGED a pillow to my chest and crossed my legs, loving Daisy's new couch. "Today was perfect."

Daisy leaned forward. "Soooo, I have a few questions. When are you going to see him next? Has he used the L word? Any mention of wedding bells?" She touched her fingers as she ticked off questions.

I imitated her actions as I answered. "He's picking me up and making me breakfast in the morning. At. His. House. He has used the L word. Yesterday when he gave me a treetop angel. She's holding a heart. He said it was to remind me that he loves me." I touched my ring finger. "But no mention of wedding bells."

She grinned. "Yet."

"We'll see, but I'm hoping. Who would've thought this is how it would turn out? I accidentally drop sparkly undies in a restaurant and meet the man of my dreams. You cannot repeat that to anyone!"

"Your secret is safe with me."

"His family is so sweet. His nieces adore him, especially the youngest." I leaned back. "I asked Javi about his firefighter housemate. But he's nearly engaged. So setting you up is out of the question."

Daisy shrugged. "No biggie. I'm fine. One day a cowboy will take me out on an exciting first date and sweep me off my feet."

I could see her with a rugged type. "And then you'd have so much to blog about."

She laughed. "You aren't wrong about that. What are the two of you doing for Christmas?"

"We're spending Christmas Eve with his family and Christmas day with mine." I stifled a yawn.

"Has there been any mention of the fact that y'all live in two different cities?"

"All the time, but never anything about how to change it. But I am working on a plan. If I tell you, you cannot breathe a word."

She ran a finger along her lips.

"It's not like there aren't banks everywhere. I applied for three jobs in this part of San Antonio. Resumes were submitted on Friday. I don't expect to hear back all that soon because things are slow for that sort of thing around the holidays, but keep your fingers crossed for me."

"Why are you keeping it a secret? Wouldn't he be excited about the idea?"

"I think he'd be ecstatic, but what if I don't get the jobs?"

Pointing at me, she waggled a finger. "Keeping secrets is a bad idea."

"It's not a secret. It's a surprise." Justification was my middle name.

CHAPTER 10

JAVI

I was more than a little excited about Bella seeing my house. Hopefully, she would like it. Otherwise, I'd have to consider changes. Big ones. And while I wasn't opposed to change, staying in San Antonio and not selling my house was my first choice.

She leaned forward in her seat as we turned onto my cul-de-sac. "This is such a nice neighborhood. I love all the trees."

"The houses have been here a while, so the trees have had years and years to grow." I parked in my driveway. "This is it."

"It has a red door!" She jumped out and ran toward the house.

Her enthusiasm for little things charmed me. I loved that about her.

"We should get you a green wreath. That would be so pretty."

The idea of hanging a wreath on my door made me laugh. With two bachelors living here, a wreath had never been part of the holiday décor. "Sure. Decorate however you want."

She squeezed my hand as I unlocked the door. "Please tell me you at least have a tree up."

"I plan to hang Christmas lights out front. Does that count for anything?"

Bella shrugged off her coat. "But you spend all day at home. Don't you want a bit of Christmas cheer?" She glanced around. "I thought you said your housemate had dogs."

"He does. They don't spend much time here anymore. He takes them to his girlfriend's house when he goes over there. And sometimes even when he's working."

She wrapped her arms around my waist. "After a quick tour, I'll help you cook. It already smells like bacon in here."

"This is the living room. Kitchen is over there. Upstairs is a second master and a den, which is Adam's space." I led her down the hall. "My office and bedroom are this way."

Her eyes went wide when she stepped into my office. The arrangement of large monitors drew her attention. "This is amazing. It's like mission control in here."

"Not exactly like that, but it works for what I do." I kissed the top of her head. "My bedroom isn't much to look at. Just a bed and a dresser. And the other bedroom is mostly empty."

"Empty? No guest room or anything like that?"

"My family all lives in town. I had no need for a guest room." I pulled her close. "I'm glad Daisy lives close, but I would've slept on the sofa if you'd wanted to stay here."

Her eyes twinkled. "Daisy would never forgive me if I stayed here instead of her place."

"I figured as much. Hungry? I'll let the cooked bacon warm in the oven while the waffles cook."

"What can I do?"

"I have strawberries, chocolate chips, and other assorted toppings . . . if you want to prep those."

"I can do that." She laced her fingers with mine. "I love your house."

That was hopeful.

I set her up with a cutting board and knife, and she sliced the ripe red berries as I ladled batter into the waffle iron. My mom had almost every kitchen gadget known to man, and I knew that heart-shaped waffles would put a smile on Bella's face.

Laughing and chatting about last night, Bella and I worked side by side making breakfast. This was what I wanted. She was who I wanted.

When I set the plate of waffles on the table, she grinned. "Hearts! You don't hang a wreath on your door, but you have a heart-shaped waffle maker? Really?" She dropped into her chair. "I never would have guessed."

"I borrowed it from my mom. But I might have to buy one to keep here."

"Maybe. It's cute. I like it." She piled strawberries on top of her waffles, added a drizzle of syrup, then topped it all with a dusting of powdered sugar. "Thank you for making breakfast. I didn't realize you could cook."

"It's nice having you here. After we eat, why don't we drive out to Comfort or another small town? We can even see if there are any geocaches out that way."

"Whatever you want to do is fine with me. I'm just happy we're spending time together." She set her fork down. "What did your family say about me? I'm guessing you've talked to them since we left the house last night."

I shifted my foot and bumped hers. "You guessed right. I fielded calls last night and this morning. My sister couldn't believe I was dating someone so pretty. Not sure what that says about her opinion of me. And my mom called me three times. She wants you to come for Christmas Eve."

Bella flashed a wide grin. "Let's eat so we can go. And I like how geocaching has become our thing."

I leaned over and kissed her. "Me too." And now I had the perfect idea for how to pop the question.

∼

I LEANED back in the booth, laughing as Daisy told yet another story about Bella.

Bella snuggled closer and turned those big brown eyes on me. "Maybe we shouldn't have invited her to join us for dinner."

"I love hearing stories about you."

"Some of these are seriously embarrassing, and I wouldn't let her tell them to just anybody."

If Daisy hadn't been sitting across the table, I would have kissed Bella after that last comment. "Now I feel special."

"You are." She tapped my arm. "Let me out. I need to run to the ladies' room."

I dutifully did as I was told.

Daisy glanced over her shoulder as Bella walked away, then leaned forward and slid a card across the table. "I wanted you to have my number in case you ever need anything. Since we live in the same town and all." She looked back again.

Staring at the card on the table, I tried to understand why Daisy was giving me her number. I'd only seen her a few times since the night I met Bella, but Daisy had never come on to me or acted weird. My hand hovered over the card as I decided what to say. "Okay, well..."

She slapped a hand over her mouth. "Oh no, I just realized how that probably sounded to you. What I mean is, if you ever need any help surprising Bella for *any particular reason*, call me. I will help. I wasn't trying to get you to call me when she wasn't around or anything like that."

"Whew! Thanks for clearing that up." I slipped her card

into my wallet. "I'll call you soon. I will need some help surprising her."

"Before Christmas?"

I gave a quick nod, then slid out of the booth as Bella approached the table. "Would you ladies like dessert?"

They looked at each other, exchanging silent words I didn't understand. "Yes." They answered in unison.

Daisy seemed to know Bella better than anyone else, so having Daisy as a helper was great. Hopefully, she could keep my secret.

CHAPTER 11

BELLA

After a full day of interviews, I leaned against the counter in Daisy's kitchen. "I didn't expect any of the jobs to respond before Christmas, but doing three interviews in one day? What was I thinking?"

"Does he know you're in town?" She added peppermint syrup to a glass full of ice, then poured in club soda. After mixing the drink, she finished it off with a splash of half-and-half. "Your peppermint soda."

"Thanks. I love the way you make Italian sodas. And this kind is my favorite."

"I bought a new bottle of peppermint syrup when you told me you were coming. And don't ignore my question."

"No, Javi doesn't know I'm here. We aren't getting together this weekend because he has something going on. Well, he said that maybe on Sunday he'd drive up to Austin. He'll call me." Bummed that I wasn't getting to see him, I was even more frustrated that I didn't know why he was busy. Curiosity burned inside my brain.

"What's with the frown? I know you miss him, but you aren't worried, right?"

"About Javi? I'm not worried." I didn't want to admit my hope and then be wrong, but I did it anyway. "I'm afraid to hope that he's busy planning a special question. That's all I want for Christmas."

"You sound pretty sure about that." She pushed a straw into her glass. "Let's sit on the sofa. Grab the macarons. The peppermint ones are soooo good. The earl grey flavor is my favorite though."

I popped a cookie in my mouth, then carried the plate to the living room. "I'm very sure that I love Javi. And even if these jobs don't work out, I want him to know that I am working on moving to San Antonio."

"You haven't told him?"

"No. I haven't told my family either. I'm not quite sure how that news will go over."

She made a face that didn't give me warm fuzzies. "Yeah, that won't be fun. Stealing away the baby of the family might get Javi in trouble."

"Gosh, I hope nobody says anything horrible like that. He has a great house in a nice neighborhood. It's not even all that far from here."

"I vote for moving. It's a win-win. Closer to me. Closer to Javi."

After a big sip of my peppermint cream soda, I leaned back. "That's what I want. But I don't want to talk about any of that right now. Have you met anyone new?"

Daisy shook her head. "No, but work stuff is going well. I'm hoping that either this spring or maybe even during the summer I can tour a local ranch and get pictures of the barn and cattle—all that good stuff."

"Ranch hands, cowboys. Those sorts of things?"

She danced her eyebrows. "Maybe a few. Sightseeing at its finest. I need to call around, but this is the wrong time of year for that."

"Let me know. I'll keep my fingers crossed that you find yourself a cowboy."

"I'll be there for work, not scoping out men."

"Right. Sure." I picked up another cookie, trying not to wonder about what Javi was doing tomorrow. My phone rang at that very moment. "It's Javi."

She laughed. "Talk to him. I'm going to take a shower."

"Hi. I miss you." I snuggled into the corner of the sofa. "How was your day?"

"Pretty good. I rearranged my schedule a bit. Are you available Saturday evening and Sunday?"

"Totally and completely available." I was anything but subtle.

He chuckled. "Good to hear."

Lightbulbs went off in my head. "What if I meet you in San Antonio?" That would be easy since I was already here.

Javi was quiet for several seconds. "Sure. If you want."

"I want. You always drive to see me. It's my turn."

"I'll call when my meeting is wrapped up and I'm back at the house. Love you."

"Love you too."

I ran down the hall. "I'm seeing him tomorrow night. I told him I'd meet him in San Antonio." Thankfully, before I opened Daisy's door, I remembered she was taking a shower. There was no one around to listen to my good news.

I shot off a text to Javi: *I'm so excited. I can't wait until tomorrow night.*

Me too. He followed his message with a heart.

CHAPTER 12

JAVI

I pulled in a deep breath, studying the menu and trying to decide what my nervous stomach could stand. Knowing Bella was in San Antonio made it harder to be in Austin, but this breakfast meeting was important.

"Mr. Morgan, thank you for—"

Bella's dad put his hand up. "Call me Paul."

"Sure. Paul, thanks for meeting with me and for switching to breakfast."

He closed his menu and pushed it toward the edge of the table. "I'm glad you called me."

"I love your daughter. And I want to ask her to be my wife." I relaxed when Mr. Morgan smiled.

"I figured that would come up. You have my blessing. Nancy and I are excited for both of you. Bella talks about you all the time."

Ordering would be easier now. With her parents' blessing, I wasn't as nervous anymore.

"She's amazing."

The waitress stepped up, and we ordered.

Mr. Morgan sipped his coffee. "I'm glad Bella found

someone grown up and settled. You'll be a good balance for her."

"She's been good for me." My thoughts jumped to my plans for the evening. I couldn't wait to pop the question.

Plates loaded with breakfast foods appeared on the table. Paul and I chatted as we ate.

He waved the waitress over and lifted his coffee cup. "We love having both girls here in Austin. Family is so important." Smiling, he paused as the waitress filled his cup.

Suddenly, I had a headache. I could tell where the conversation was headed, and his comments were unexpected. Bella had been more than clear about how she loved my house. We hadn't discussed her moving to San Antonio, but I'd planned to bring it up tonight.

"So, tell me. When are you planning to move to Austin? Before the wedding?"

"Bella and I haven't talked about that." I poked at my scrambled eggs. "We'll discuss all that after I propose."

"Of course." He picked up his fork. "I just didn't want you stealing my little girl away to a different city."

I smiled. So much for enjoying breakfast.

AFTER CHUGGING A BLUEBERRY IZZE, I texted Daisy. *Everything is ready.*

Right now, I didn't want to think about moving or about stealing Bella away from her family. Tonight was about making Bella smile. There was no doubt how she'd answer my question. And there would be time later to sort out the details about life after the wedding.

If Bella chose to stay in Austin, I'd move in a heartbeat. And I might even set that in motion before we talked about it. If her father felt so strongly about keeping family close, Bella probably did too.

When Daisy had called and told me Bella was spending the weekend in San Antonio, I'd shifted plans.

Now that it was almost time to pick Bella up, excitement threatened to choke me. I'd never wanted anything so much in my entire life.

I checked that the champagne was chilling in the fridge and set the vase of roses in the center of the table. Thankfully, the dogs weren't here.

As soon as Daisy arrived and I gave her what she needed for the surprise, the plan would be set in motion.

A knock startled me out of my thoughts, and I yanked open the door.

Daisy clapped. "She is going to flip."

"Thanks for helping."

"Of course! Now give me the stuff so you can go see her."

I handed over the instructions I'd carefully typed out and a small box. "Please don't lose that."

"Wouldn't dream of it." She laughed. "See you in a bit." Waving, she ran to her car.

Before she'd pulled away from the curb, I was in the truck, eager to pick up Bella.

CHAPTER 13

BELLA

I'd changed clothes three times.

Pacing, I checked the time. "He said evening. It's four. When do you think evening officially starts?"

"I think you're nuts." Daisy pulled on a black sweatshirt. With an all-black outfit, she looked like a cat burglar. "Are y'all going geocaching?" She was making fun of me.

"Where are you going dressed like that? Headed out to scale a building and steal precious jewels?" I poked back. That's what friends were for.

"Funny. Not." She flashed a tight-lipped grin. "I have a thing. Text me and let me know how your evening goes. You have a key. Come and go as you please." Daisy waved, then hurried out the door.

How could she just leave when I was pacing impatiently? Who would distract me?

After another fifteen minutes of pacing, my phone rang. "Hello?"

"Hey there." Javi's deep smooth voice echoed through the line. "Did I catch you at a good time?"

"I could pretend I was super busy, but truly, I've been

waiting for your call. I'm at Daisy's. Do you want me to come to your house?"

"I'll come pick you up. The River Walk is decked out with lights. I thought maybe we'd have dinner down there and then stroll for a bit."

"That sounds perfect."

"I'll be there in five minutes." He sounded like he was already in the car.

After slipping on my shoes and coat, I checked the geocaching site. Maybe we'd find a cache along the River Walk.

JAVI and I walked out of the restaurant. With my arm looped around his, I snuggled close, glad the weather was only mildly chilly.

"Good food. Good company. Tonight has been perfect." I smiled up at him. "I'm glad I got to see you."

He chewed his bottom lip a second before answering. "Me too. You look beautiful tonight."

"Thanks! Earlier, I looked on the website. There are a few geocaches down here along the river."

He reached into his pocket. "It's a good thing I brought along trinkets."

I opened the app. "There's one not far from here."

"Lead the way." His smile seriously threatened to melt my heart.

We didn't walk far before we arrived at the coordinates. Next to a bench, near the base of a tree was a small canister.

He opened it up and dumped the contents into his hand. "What do you want to take?"

"This." I picked up a sparkly unicorn figurine. "I think I need a tiny unicorn."

He signed the logbook, then tossed a trinket into the cache before putting it back where we found it. "Any others?"

I checked the app for our next destination. I scanned the list of caches in the area, then froze. "We need to find this one. It's called the Sparkly cache. It wasn't listed earlier. I would've noticed."

"Which way?"

I stared at the map, getting my bearings. "That way."

We walked—actually, it probably looked more like I was dragging Javi down the sidewalk. Finding a cache named Sparkly seemed serendipitous.

Almost out of breath, I stopped at the base of a staircase. "It should be around here somewhere." I scanned the ground, but the darkness made it hard to see.

Javi turned on his flashlight. "Did it give any clues?"

I checked the app again. "Look up. The future is bright."

"I wonder what that means." He leaned over my shoulder. "Any ideas?"

"Shine your light up there. It's in the tree, I bet."

He pointed his flashlight at the trunk of the tree and moved the light upward.

I nearly dove toward the tree when I spotted the sparkly box. "They weren't kidding. This is sparkly."

Javi moved behind me as I lifted the lid off the box.

The lid hit the ground as I grabbed for the tiny little velvet box nestled inside the bigger one.

"Are you going to sign the logbook?" He handed me the little book and took the sparkly box.

I opened to the first page of the little book and read the inscription.

Bella, will you marry me?

CHAPTER 14

JAVI

As Bella spun to face me, I dropped to one knee. "Bella, I had no idea I needed sparkle in my life until I met you. You make my life sparkly. Will you marry me?"

With the ring box still clutched to her chest, she nodded, tears pooling in her eyes. "Yes!"

I held out my hand. "Why don't we open the box?"

Her hands shook as she handed it to me. "I almost forgot about the ring. I was so excited about the question."

I slipped the solitaire out of the cushion and slid it onto her finger. "I love you, Bella."

She threw her arms around me. "I'm so happy. So very happy. I love you so much."

Tonight was for celebrating.

"How did you manage this? Please tell me you didn't leave this here, trusting that no one else would find it during dinner."

Bushes rustled behind us, and Daisy jumped out. "Surprise!"

Bella hugged her friend. "You sneak!"

"I caught it all on video." Daisy hugged me. "I'll send it to both of you. Congratulations. I'm so excited. I have a whole stash of bridal magazines at my house we can look through later."

Bella clapped.

I tucked an arm around Bella's waist and held out my arm to Daisy. "Let's all go to my house and celebrate with a glass of champagne."

Walking down the sidewalk, they chatted about possible wedding dates and colors.

"What do you think?" Bella glanced up at me.

"You can choose whatever colors you want. And I'm flexible on dates. Seeing you walk up the aisle is what's important to me." I kissed the top of her head.

"This is the best Christmas ever." Bella wiped her eyes.

Daisy laughed. "Christmas is a week away."

"And it'll be so busy at work. Ugh." Bella shook her head. "People go nuts right before Christmas."

"Don't think about that right now. Let's enjoy tonight."

"Good advice."

Back at the house, we sipped champagne while Bella and Daisy tossed wedding ideas back and forth.

"February?" Bella looked at me, her eyebrows raised.

I pointed at the calendar. "Any weekend except this one. I need to attend a wedding, and I'll need a date."

"I'd love to go with you." She kissed my cheek. "We should plan ours for the weekend after. Wouldn't it be funny if you caught the garter?"

"I'll do my best."

∼

Sunday Bella and I visited a few venues between San Antonio and Austin. Being in separate cars gave us less time to chat, but soon, she'd have to drive home.

We walked out of a cute, rustic venue.

"I loved that place. It's the perfect size, don't you think?"

"I do." I glanced at the time.

It was almost time to say goodbye.

If I didn't bring up where to live now, I'd lose my chance because I didn't want to discuss it over the phone. "I was thinking. After the wedding—"

She glanced at her phone when it rang. "I'm sorry. It's my mom."

"Answer it." I listened as she recounted every detail of the venues to her mom.

Perhaps after Christmas, we'd have more time to talk.

CHAPTER 15

BELLA

My car loaded with presents for Javi's family, I parked in his driveway. The plan was for him to pick me up early tomorrow, but I opted for a surprise.

Seeing his truck in the driveway gave me hope that he was home, easing my worry that my surprise would go awry.

I knocked. Footsteps sounded, then the knob rattled. Finally, the door opened. "Bella!"

"Surprise. I took the afternoon off, so I figured I'd drive down early. I hope that's okay."

"More than okay. Come in." He stepped back to let me in, then glanced down at his sweats and ratty t-shirt. "As you can see, I wasn't expecting company."

I threw my arms around his neck. "You look absolutely huggable."

"Just huggable?" He tugged me toward the sofa.

I dropped into his lap. "Maybe kissable." Loving the feel of his stubble against my palms, I danced my lips on his. "And I have a surprise for you. I was going to wait until Christmas, but I can't."

His eyes narrowed. "Okay?" He had the ability to restrain his excitement and curiosity, a skill I lacked.

A knock sounded, and I shifted out of his lap.

"Hold that thought." He pulled open the door. "Hi, Marisa. What's up?"

"I'm just dropping off comps for the area. These will help us determine the asking price if you decide to sell."

Sell?

I couldn't let him do that. In a second, I was behind him. With my arms snaked around his waist, I leaned around and smiled at the Realtor. "We like this house. I doubt he wants to sell it. I mean, it is his house, and the decision will ultimately be his, but I don't think . . ." I'd just embarrassed myself. I buried my face in Javi's back. "Sorry."

He reached back and tugged me next to him. "Bella, this is Marisa Torres, the Realtor. But I think you already figured out that last part. Marisa, this is my fiancée, Bella Morgan."

"Nice to meet you, Bella." The Marisa woman smiled. "I'll go so the two of you can talk. And if you decide not to list the house, that's fine. It is a great neighborhood. I can understand why you'd want to stay." She turned and walked back to her car.

Javi closed the door and slowly turned to face me. "That was going to be my surprise. I called a Realtor."

"You succeeded in surprising me."

"In the same way you'd be surprised by a snake in the grass."

"Pretty much." I clasped his hand and dragged him back to the couch. "Sit."

Laugh lines creased near his eyes. "Am I going to be scolded?"

I nestled back into his lap. "I really want to tell you my surprise, but first we have to deal with this Realtor thing.

Why would you even think of selling this house? I love this place."

"Just to be clear, I planned to discuss it with you before listing it, but after talking to your dad—"

"When did you talk to my dad?"

"We had breakfast Saturday morning. I asked for his blessing before we went downtown."

"Please tell me he gave it. Because if he didn't, I'm going to have a word with him. I've made no secret of the fact that I love you."

"He gave his blessing. But he also asked when I was moving to Austin because he didn't want me stealing his little girl away to a different city."

It wasn't enough that I could embarrass myself, my family had to do it too. I should've warned Javi about my dad. "Here's the thing. My dad is a little . . . um . . ." I trailed a finger down his t-shirt as I figured out what to say. "When Martha was close to graduating from college, Dad bought her a house so that she wouldn't move away. She was already working for his company part time. He likes having us in the same town. But I refused to take a job at his company, and I wouldn't let him buy me a house."

"So your dad is hoping I'll make you stay in Austin."

"Make me?"

He laughed and pulled me in for a kiss.

When we broke the kiss, I sprang my news. "I gave notice at work. The second week of January, I start work at the bank that's a mile down the road. It's a promotion for me, and better pay."

He blinked. "Are you sure?"

"It's what I want. And I would've asked you, but if I made the choice alone, nobody could blame you."

His fingers threaded into my hair, and he sealed his lips to mine. Again. I'd never get tired of kissing him.

As I leaned closer, his arms tightened around me. My heart thumped in rhythm with his, and all the world was right. "I love you, Javi."

"And your parents will hate me."

"But they'll get over it." I kissed his cheek, relishing the prickle of his whiskers. "I hope you know I'm joking. They won't hate you."

"Even if they do, my priority is your happiness. If you want to move to San Antonio, I'll support you all the way." He brushed a finger along my cheek. "I'll even use my truck to help you move."

"Yay. And I was hoping, if it's not too big an imposition . . ." I paused and chuckled at his quizzical expression. "I'm going to move in with Daisy until the wedding. I know we haven't even officially set a date, but still. Can I store all my extra stuff in the empty bedroom?"

He nodded. "Anything you need."

"So, what were you planning to do with your evening?"

"Wrap gifts. Want to help?"

I cradled his face. "Whatever you need."

CHAPTER 16

JAVI

Christmas Eve with my family had gone just as I'd expected. Everyone was excited about the engagement, and when Bella announced that we'd be living in San Antonio, my mom cried.

I had a feeling her mom would do the same thing but for a different reason.

That thought put a damper on my Christmas cheer, but I didn't want Bella to know that. Standing in her kitchen, I poured myself a cup of coffee and prepped one for her.

Her bedroom door opened. "Tell me again why I agreed to be at Martha's house at six in the morning. Ugh, It's early."

I handed her a mug. "It is, but think of Natalie and Nathan. They'll be so excited that Santa came."

"I know." She rubbed her eyes, then blinked. "What are you wearing?"

"You don't like my Christmas pajamas?"

"It looks like a giant onesie." She slapped a hand to her mouth. "You look . . ."

"Ridiculous?"

"Maybe a little." She set her coffee on the counter and

wrapped her arms around me. "But I love that you are participating in our tradition."

"I bought you a matching pair." I pointed at the neatly wrapped box on the table.

Giggling, she tore off the paper. "Martha is going to flip when we show up in matching PJs. She and Owen wore coordinated stuff for the first few years they were married. It was soooo cute." Bella rolled her eyes. "But they haven't done it in a while. Owen may be a tad irritated with you for this."

"I'll just make your entire family mad all in one day." I joked about it, but it was a real fear.

"Don't worry, Javi. It'll be fine." She downed the rest of her coffee. "Let me change, then we'll go."

CRADLING A LARGE MUG OF COFFEE, Bella snuggled beside me as the kids opened gifts. Bright-colored wrapping paper covered the floor, and laughter echoed off the walls.

Owen walked up carrying the carafe. "Refill? Caffeine is the only thing keeping me going right now."

"Please." I held out my empty mug. "I hope our matching pajamas don't cause you grief in the future."

"Yeah. Thanks for that. I think I'm doomed to matching PJs next Christmas. That is, if this happens next year." His voice was low, but the tinge of concern in it was unmistakable.

We hadn't given our news, so what was Owen talking about?

Once the kiddos had opened all their gifts and were busy playing, the adults passed around presents.

One by one, gifts were unwrapped. And all the while, I waited for the news to break. But even after the last gift had been opened, there still hadn't been any mention of moving to Austin. After the initial flurry of congratulations when we'd arrived, they hadn't said anything else about the engagement or the wedding.

Trying not to think about all that, I stuffed ribbons and paper into a trash bag.

Bella walked up and rubbed my back. "Come to the table. We're ready to eat. You don't have to clean this up."

"Are we going to tell them today?"

"I am." She inched up and brushed her lips on mine. "Relax. It'll be fine."

I hugged her close. "I'm going to trust you on that."

"Good."

We sat down at the table just as Martha ran out of the room.

Owen glanced down the hall. "Let me go check on her."

Bella scanned the table, and her eyes widened. Under the table, she clasped my hand. "It was the orange juice. I bet I'm going to be an aunt again."

Mrs. Morgan crossed her fingers. "What other explanation is there?"

"More family to love. I'm glad they're all close." Mr. Morgan knew how to rain on my parade.

Martha walked back to the table, gripping Owen's hand. "Sorry to keep you waiting."

Bella jumped up. "I'm moving to San Antonio, but I'll still come visit."

Was this what she'd planned the whole time? Because this didn't seem like the best way to break the news.

My thought was confirmed when Martha ran from the room with tears streaming down her face.

Mrs. Morgan slapped a hand to her chest, and Mr. Morgan pushed back from the table and walked out of the room.

Bella sat down and grabbed my hand. "I probably could have done that better."

Without a clue what to say that could make the situation better, I kissed her hand. Ruining Christmas wasn't how I wanted today to go.

Mrs. Morgan smiled. "I'm not surprised. I've been expecting this announcement for a while."

Bella sighed. "I didn't know how to tell you. I applied for a job in San Antonio. They hired me, and I'll be moving in January."

Her dad appeared in the doorway, his gaze fixed on me.

"Dad, you can't blame Javi. I didn't talk to him about moving until after I'd accepted the job."

Her mom grinned and extended a hand toward her husband. "We are so happy for both of you. When I moved to Austin from Houston, my parents didn't speak to Paul for a month. Eventually, they came around and forgave him. We'd never do that to you. Isn't that right, Paul?"

Mr. Morgan sat down in his chair. "As long as you visit."

I nodded. "We'll visit."

Maybe Christmas wouldn't end in a disaster.

Owen wrapped his arms around Martha as they stepped up to the table. "Our good news, as you've probably already guessed, is that baby number three is on the way. The bad news is, we're moving to Houston at the beginning of March. My job is being shifted to a different office."

Mr. Morgan pulled the foil off the casserole, much calmer than I would've expected after that last announcement. "Looks like I'm going to have to retire. I guess we're moving to Houston. What do you think, Nancy?"

"I'll start looking for a house."

He glanced at Bella. "I hope you don't mind."

"Not in the least. You should be near the grandkids." She

kissed my cheek and lowered her voice. "See, I told you not to worry."

There at the table, dressed in ridiculous green pajamas, I fell in love all over again with the sparkly wonder who made the world a better place. "Bella Morgan, I love you."

"Good." She brushed her lips on my ear. "When you look at me that way, it makes my toes tingle. And they aren't cold because these are footed pajamas."

And now I wanted to kiss her.

"Javi, will you pass the biscuits?" Mr. Morgan's timing probably wasn't an accident.

I handed the basket down the table, then snuck a quick kiss from Bella. "Merry Christmas."

"This is the best one yet."

After a stop at Bella's apartment to change out of our Christmas jammies, we were on the road to Johnson City for our planned getaway. Two days alone with my fiancée sounded like pure bliss.

She shifted in her seat and crossed her legs. "Okay. I know we've only been engaged less than a week, but there are a few things I think we should talk about."

I reached for her hand. "And what's that?"

"I've been thinking. I don't really want a wedding, a big fancy one." She squeezed my hand. "Would you be too disappointed if we just had a small ceremony for our families? Maybe even in your backyard."

Not spending thousands of dollars on a wedding sounded fine to me, not that I wouldn't have spent it in a heartbeat if Bella had wanted a fancy shindig. "A backyard wedding sounds perfect."

"I hoped that you'd like the idea. The other thing—since

I'm staying with the same company and transferring to a different branch—I have lots of vacation time saved up, but I'll be in training until mid-February, so I can't take the vacation time until then. I explained to them that I'd be taking some time off after my wedding."

"Then I think February sounds like a great time to get married." I kissed her fingers. "What else should we talk about?"

"Kids." She bit her lower lip.

I brushed my thumb across the side of her hand. "Bella, I want to marry *you*. No matter how you feel about having kids, I want to spend my life with you."

"Do you want kids?"

"I want you." When she'd told her dad that they should live near the grandkids, I'd considered the idea that maybe she didn't plan to have children.

"You said that, but I want to know your answer. Please." Why had she brought this up when I couldn't pull her into my lap and watch her reaction as I answered?

"Yes, I'd like to be a dad one day." Honesty was the foundation of all strong relationships. And I learned this morning that trusting her was always a good idea.

She turned and looked out the window. "Is there a spot where you can pull off the road for a minute?"

"Yeah. Hang on." I scanned both sides of the road for a pull off. With her face hidden from view, I couldn't see her expression.

Worry thumped in my head.

A second later an empty parking lot came into view. I turned in and parked. "Bella?"

Wiping her eyes, she unbuckled her seatbelt and crawled over the center console. "I really want to kiss you right now. I would've married you no matter what you wanted, but I really do want children. And you'll be an awesome dad." She wedged herself into my lap, honking the horn in the process.

"You had me scared for a minute."

Her lips caught mine, and conversation halted for several seconds. When she pulled back, she trailed a finger through my whiskers. "I just don't want kids right away."

"I like that plan." I pulled her in for another kiss. "A backyard wedding in February, huh?"

"Too soon?"

"Not at all." I chuckled as she climbed back into her seat.

Grinning, she buckled her seatbelt. "You can drive now."

I had the ability, but not the desire. "I'm not in a hurry. Why don't you come back over here for a bit?"

She released the seatbelt and shifted back into my lap. "It's probably a good thing this shop is closed. Because otherwise, we'd be attracting unwanted attention."

"There's no law against kissing. At least I don't think there is."

With her arms snaked around my neck, she brushed her lips on mine before kissing me so passionately, it made my toes tingle.

When she pulled back, I sighed. "Wow. Merry Christmas to me."

She laughed. "I love you too. Now, let's go see those spectacular lights."

EPILOGUE

BELLA

At Adam's wedding, I leaned against Javi as the single ladies were called out to the floor. "I'm giving myself an exemption."

He winked. "I'd hate for you to mess up that dress tackling another woman to get the bouquet."

We laughed when the redhead who caught the prized bouquet scanned the room.

"She's looking for someone."

Javi pointed to a handsome man leaning against the wall in the shadows. "And someone is looking at her."

The deejay called for the single men to go out to the floor.

"I'll be back . . . with the garter."

"Don't hurt anyone."

He laughed.

The men lined up, and when Adam tossed the blue lacy garter, several guys dove to catch it. Javi snagged it out of the air and stepped back as others fell over each other.

Clapping, I grinned as my love walked back toward the table.

He dropped into the chair next to me and handed me the garter. "I caught it."

"You're so fun! And you totally took out the other guys doing it."

He shrugged. "When you want something, I will always do my best to make it happen."

With Javi, I felt loved and cared for. I leaned my head on his shoulder. "Look the redhead is sitting with the guy who was watching her. See the way he's looking at her?"

"What about it?"

"I bet it's making her toes tingle." I kissed Javi's cheek. "How am I going to wait until next weekend? Think our families would be too upset if we hopped a plane for Vegas and got married tonight?" I'd started the question as a joke, but hearing it out loud increased my desire to do just that. "There's no law against marrying the same person twice, right?"

He gave me the look that made my toes tingle. "You're off all week?"

"This coming week and next."

Staring at me, he chewed his bottom lip. "How long will it take you to pack?"

"Fifteen minutes."

His lips pressed to mine. "Let's give our congratulations to the happy couple, then I'll book our flight."

Six hours later, still dressed up from the wedding, we stepped off the plane in Las Vegas.

Javi flagged down a taxi. "First item of business—getting a marriage license."

I glanced out the window at the night sky. "They'll be closed."

He laughed. "That is probably true in any other city, but here, they are open until midnight every night. I filled out the application during the flight. And I booked the last slot at a wedding chapel."

"When did you do all that?"

He grinned. "While you were sleeping."

After signing paperwork, we rushed to the chapel. After a short ceremony, Javi carried me out to an awaiting limo. "Mrs. Martinez, your carriage awaits."

"Right now, I truly feel like a princess. One who is getting away with something." I snuggled beside him in the back of the limo and trailed a finger along his ring band. "Did you also book us a room?"

"I did."

"When are we going to tell our families?"

"Tomorrow, we can send them all a picture of our rings. Tonight, I have other plans."

Heat flooded my cheeks.

The limousine stopped in front of a hotel. Fountains accented with lights danced as we stepped out into the night.

Javi escorted me into the hotel. "Let me check in really quick."

"I'll be right back." I slipped into the ladies' room.

Staring into the mirror, I thought of the night when I'd splashed water on my legs to get rid of the static. Look where that had gotten me.

I hurried out and found Javi.

Holding our bags, he grinned. "Ready?" The question was full of excitement and promise . . . a promise of little sleep.

"Very."

The elevator doors closed, and Javi kissed me until they opened again. He led me to the room, then swiped the room key.

As he dropped the bags, I dropped something else. They weren't sparkly. Lacy would be a better description.

He gave a low rumble of a chuckle. "You dropped something."

"Did I?" I fluttered my lashes.

Instead of picking up what I'd dropped, he picked me up. "Please tell me you were dropping hints."

I undid his top button. "I want you."

Javi made it clear he wanted me too.

What a perfect way to begin our happily ever after.

If you want to read about Adam and his girlfriend, grab a copy of *Three Things I'd Never Do*.

A NOTE TO READERS

Thank you for reading!

After Javi showed up in *Three Things I'd Never Do*, I had a couple of readers ask if he'd get his own story. Since he hadn't ever actually made it to the page, I hadn't considered a story for him. All we knew about Javi was that he was out of town almost every weekend to visit his girlfriend.

A Christmas novella seemed like the perfect way to give him his own story. And geocaching popped into my head (something I haven't done in years!) so I worked that into the story.

CHRISTMAS SURPRISE

A mistakenly sent text reunites two people who weren't expecting love.

CHAPTER 1

JOSEFINA

This was one of those nights where the voices in my head didn't agree. One side was excited to be getting out of the house. The other side scolded me for wanting to feel young. My friend Joji wasn't that much younger than I was, but she had twice my youth. Maybe a little was rubbing off on me.

"Ay, ay, ay!" Or maybe not. If I was too old to use a smart phone, maybe I was too old to go dancing.

"What?" My new friend Joji laughed. "If you're nervous, don't be. We'll have fun."

"I was trying to let my daughter know where we were going tonight, but I accidentally texted someone I haven't spoken to in ten years." My cheeks burned as I tapped out another message. *Oops. Wrong person. Sorry.*

"What did you tell him? And two more questions. Is he good looking and single? How do you have a number from ten years ago?"

"When I get a new phone, my boys move everything over just like Jeffrey used to do. I think I still have their little league coach's number in this thing." I sent off a text to my daughter, triple checking that I was sending it to the right person. "I told him where we were going dancing." I hadn't quite worded it that way, but I wasn't going to admit to the actual text I sent. "And yes, he's good looking, but last time I talked to him, he was happily married."

"How long ago was that?"

"Ten years ago. He was at my brother's retirement party. They were partners on the force for years." I glanced out the window as the Lyft driver stopped in front of the building with a bright neon sign. "I hope I don't regret letting you talk me into this."

"It's one night. We'll have a drink, dance a little, then go home. It'll be great." Joji ran her fingers through her curls. "I'm going to find a cowboy who will twirl me around the dance floor."

"I'm going to watch others dance." I had no plans to get out on the dance floor.

"Find a table with my name on it. I reserved one. I'll grab drinks." Joji nudged me forward. "I won't be long."

I strolled by tables, reading the names on the reserved signs. Not far from the bar, I found Joji's table. After shrugging off my coat, I hopped onto the barstool. The tall tables made it easier to see with all the people standing around.

"Your margarita, my dear." Joji sat a glass in front of me then spun around, her dress twirling around her. "I wore my dancing dress tonight."

"I wore my sitting jeans." I hadn't worn these tight-fitted jeans in years. Shockingly, they still fit. "How did I let you talk me into this?"

"When was the last time you've been out for the evening? And with your kids doesn't count."

"Not since before Jeffrey died. More than three years ago. I stay home and cook or crochet. Isn't that what grandmas are supposed to do?" I enjoyed giving my new friend a hard time.

"It's a good thing you met me." Joji sipped her margarita. "Now let's watch the floor. I want to see who can dance."

She didn't get much of a chance to watch.

A tall cowboy who looked like he'd been a bull rider in earlier years sauntered up to the table. "Evening ladies."

When he tipped his hat, Joji sighed.

That only spurred him on. "Can I interest you in a spin around the dance floor?"

"You betcha." Joji hopped off her bar stool, hooked her arm around his, and flashed me a grin as they walked away.

I leaned on the table, sipping my drink. It was nice to be around people.

CHAPTER 2

MATEO

*R*etirement was supposed to be the reward after many years of work, but no one warned me how lonely it would be. Six months after my last day on the job, my wife died unexpectedly. Without anyone to spend my best years with, I often spent weeknights in front of the television.

I'd just finished off the last of my frozen pizza when my phone buzzed. Why was Eddie's sister texting me?

Two single ladies heading to The Thirsty Horse. Tonight should be fun.

Another text quickly followed. *Oops Wrong person. Sorry.*

I stared at the phone, trying to decide how to respond. Nothing clever came to mind, so I hopped off the couch, changed into jeans and a button down, and yanked on my boots. If Josefina was single and out dancing, there was no reason for me to stay home alone.

The Thirsty Horse was one of my haunts most weekends, and I knew several regulars who frequented on Thursdays also. I stepped up to the bar and waited as the bartender settled a tab. When Sally looked up, she smiled. "Evening, Mateo. The usual?"

"Please." I laid money on the counter and stuffed a tip into the jar. "It's busy tonight."

"For a Thursday, it is." She leaned over the bar and motioned toward the many people gathered in clusters. "Lots of available dance partners if you're wanting to dance."

I lifted my beer. "Thanks."

"And if you're free on my break, I'll dance with you." She winked.

"I'll never say no to that." I slipped my koozie on the bottle. That was an easy way to distinguish mine from the others that would inevitably end up sitting near my bottle.

Leaning on the end of the bar, I scanned the room.

"Looking for someone?" Spanky—he had a name, but we all called him Spanky—slapped me on the back.

"Aren't we all?"

"Not me. I'm just looking for a dance partner."

I clinked my bottle against his, then returned to my hunt.

Seated just a few feet away, Josefina sat on a bar stool, laughing as the redhead sitting at the same table waved her arms as she told a story.

After a swig, I snaked my way through the crowd. "Evening."

Josefina's hand shot to her mouth, and she giggled. The sheer delight in the sound had me smiling.

"Would you like to dance?" I set my beer on the table.

After a quick glance at my ring finger, she nodded.

"Do you really think I would've shown up here and asked you to dance if I was married?" I crossed my arms and gave her what I hoped was a mildly scolding look.

Her cheeks colored, or maybe that was a reflection from the neon. She sipped her drink before sliding off the barstool. "I haven't done this in years."

I tucked an arm around her waist as we stepped onto the dance floor. "Try not to step on my toes."

She cut off the circulation in my hand during the first few steps, but as we continued to dance, she relaxed.

When I danced us in a circle, she moved in closer, so I danced us in another circle. Her dark eyes reflected the neon lights, and she treated me to another giggle.

I'd never heard her giggle before, and I found it very entertaining.

So far, the evening was exceeding my expectations.

The song ended, and the deejay put on something slow. Josefina kept hold of my hand and smiled up at me. "I'm surprised to see you."

"Why? You told me you were here."

"You look good."

"I was about to say the same thing."

She bumped my boot then rested her head against my chest as she laughed. "I'm so sorry. One margarita is enough for me."

"Eddie hadn't mentioned you were single again." I didn't want to make presumptions about why she was single.

"Jeffrey died three years ago. Eddie also didn't mention that you were single."

"Maria died five years ago." I hadn't anticipated having this conversation on the dance floor. After twirling Josefina, I pulled her close again. "I'm sorry to hear about your husband. Eddie said he was a great guy."

She pinched her lips together and nodded. "Much better than my first."

"But we won't talk about him." I didn't like seeing her tense. I preferred her smile.

"Did you come because of the text?" Quiet, but always straightforward, Josefina's question didn't surprise me.

"I did. When I couldn't figure out what to send as a response, I decided to send myself."

She laughed and patted my chest. "You've always been funny. That hasn't changed."

Through three more songs, we stayed on the dance floor.

"I should go check on my friend."

"If you mean the redhead who was at your table, she's right behind you, dancing with Marvin. He's here almost every weekend."

Josefina glanced back over her shoulder. "Then I guess we stay out here a little longer."

Those words were music to my ears.

After several more songs, Josefina tugged me off the dance floor. "I need to sit down."

"Can I get you a fresh drink?"

"Oh no! No more alcohol for me." She hopped up on the bar stool.

I dragged over another stool, one that had been abandoned near the wall. "I can get you a Coke or water."

She rested a hand on my arm. "Water would be great."

"Coming right up."

As I walked up to the bar, Sally laughed. "I looked for you, but someone else got to you first."

I knew she wasn't flirting, and that being a regular was the reason for the banter. "Bumped into an old friend."

"Lucky lady. What can I get you to drink?"

I glanced back, and Josefina flashed a smile. "Two waters. And I think I'm the lucky one."

I'd come on a whim. Dancing had been fun. But this was different than other nights I'd spent dancing.

I carried the cups back to the table. "I'm glad for the oops text."

"Me too. This has been fun, and it's so good to see you."

"Are you free Saturday? We could have dinner then dance the night away." I drew lines in the condensation on the table. Asking out someone who I'd known forever felt like walking out on the ice in spring, not that I knew how that felt. Lakes around San Antonio never froze.

"Mateo Garza, are you asking me out?"

I looked up. "I am. This was fun."

She squeezed my hand, and I prepared for a soft let down.

"This *was* fun. And if I can walk come Saturday, I'd love to go out with you."

I trailed my thumb across her fingers. "If you can walk?"

"After tonight, my thighs are going to scream at me. Gardening did not prepare me for this." Humor glinted in her eyes.

There was a benefit to knowing someone for years. My joking wouldn't be misunderstood. "I can come over and massage them for you . . . if that will help."

She swatted my arm. "Mateo!"

Her friend walked back to the table, and Josefina pulled her hand away. "Mateo, this is my friend Joji."

"Nice to meet you, Joji."

"Same here. I worried that Josefina would spend all night people-watching from the table, but boy oh boy. I was wrong about that." She checked the time. "How have we been here so long?"

"It's almost midnight." Josefina fanned her face. "We need to call for a ride."

"Nonsense. I'll give y'all a ride home." I stepped closer to her. "If you want."

Joji didn't give Josefina a chance to answer. "That would be wonderful. What a gentleman." She hopped off her stool. "Ready?"

"Yes." Josefina picked up her coat.

I held it out so she could slip her arms in. "I'm looking forward to Saturday."

She glanced back over her shoulder. "Me too. My text was a serendipitous mistake."

CHAPTER 3

JOSEFINA

Mateo stopped in front of the house. "Well, ladies, I had a great time. Let me get those doors." He strolled around to the passenger side of the truck.

Joji jumped out and didn't turn around until she was halfway to the door. Waving, she yawned. "I'm headed in. Goodnight." Her acting skills were quite convincing.

I leaned back against the truck. "I said this already, but I had fun."

"Me too. I'll call you tomorrow to check in and see how those thighs are feeling." He moved in closer. "I'm glad you still had my number."

I reminded myself that he was lonely and wanted a friend. The man had always been handsome, and years hadn't changed that. For several seconds we stood in the dark, gazing at each other. The reminder about him wanting a friend hadn't reached my heart. It pounded hard and fast.

Resisting the urge to wrap him in a long, tight hug, I patted his chest. "How's this? I'll say yes to dinner, and we'll see how I feel before deciding on dancing."

"Sounds great." He stood beside the truck until I was inside. When I peeked around the curtain, he waved.

Joji dropped onto the sofa, already in her jammies. "Go change, then fill me in. Want tea or popcorn or something?"

"Just tea for me. I'll be out in just a few minutes." As I changed clothes, I laughed at myself. I was acting just like I did when I was young. And I hadn't felt young in a long time.

I had Joji to thank for that.

A mug of hot tea was waiting for me in the living room. She jumped right into the interrogation. "When we went out on Tuesday, you didn't dance once. Tonight? You danced with that man almost the entire time. He's a looker, for sure, but it surprised me. Are you going out with him again?"

"Yes, on Saturday. Mateo is a retired police detective. He was widowed five years ago."

"Y'all covered a lot of topics on the dance floor."

I shook my head. "I've known Mateo a long time. He was my brother's partner for years. A friend of the family." Hoping the mug would cover the secrets probably etched on my face, I sipped my tea.

Joji squinted one eye. "But he was a good friend?"

"He's the one I accidentally texted."

She squealed. "I love it already, but that didn't answer the question."

"Mateo and I have never dated." I cradled my mug, deciding that being open about my past would help me navigate this new relationship. "He was around when I was married to my first husband."

"The one who hit you?"

"Only once. My brothers—and I'm guessing Mateo, but I don't know for sure—asked him to leave town and never come back. Shortly after the divorce was final, Mateo showed up one evening and offered to marry me. We'd never gone on a date or had a romantic encounter. Not once."

"I'm guessing you said no because of Jeffrey, who became your second husband."

"I didn't meet Jeffrey for another two years. But I told Mateo no because I couldn't let him marry me out of some obligation to care for me and my daughter. It was the right thing to do. He met Maria ten months later, and they fell in love."

"Oh my." Joji fanned herself. "And now you meet again."

"I think he enjoyed the companionship. And I understand that. It'll be nice to have a friend to go dancing with."

"Careful with the word friend. It'll bite you." She laughed. "It's a good thing I dragged you out dancing!"

I kicked at her foot, shaking my head. "Tell me about your evening."

"It was fun, but I just went to dance." She crossed her legs and leaned forward. "But there is something about a man in boots."

"There is!" I finished off the rest of my tea. "One request."

"What's that?"

"Please don't say anything about my past with Mateo. I want to see where this goes before I bring up some of those things."

Joji ran a finger along her lips. "Nothing about the past. But I can mention the date, right?"

"Yes, I'm not going to keep that from Nacha. My daughter will understand. I'll tell the boys in person when they are here for Christmas if I see Mateo again after Saturday."

"It's hard to believe that's only weeks away. I'll clear out while you have family here. You need your space."

"I invited you to stay here. You don't have to leave."

She waved her hand. "Don't worry about me."

That was good because if I were the worrying type, Saturday's date would stir up enough worry to keep my brain busy all night.

~

I picked up my fork as the waitress walked away. "Everything looks so good."

"It does. So, how are your kids?" Mateo had been slow to bring up the past, but this question eased us in that direction.

"Good. The boys are both married. I'm a grandma to two little guys."

Mateo smiled without looking up. "You hardly seem old enough for that."

"I'm well past fifty."

"Hey, that's not old." He glanced up, and the twinkle in his brown eyes made me want more than friendship.

"That's what my friend Joji keeps telling me."

"And how's Nacha?" His voice softened.

I swallowed back the lump in my throat. "She's trying to work through things in her marriage. It's complicated. But overall, she's okay."

"I'm sorry I wasn't around more when she was growing up." He poked at his food.

I reached across the table and rested my hand on his. "Mateo, I never wanted Maria to be jealous. That's why I stopped inviting both of you to the house. Don't blame yourself."

"I don't know that she was jealous exactly, but after she lost the baby and it became clear that we weren't going to have children, seeing me playing with Nacha was painful."

"I'm so sorry." I squeezed his hand. "Hindsight offers a different perspective. It lets us see the past differently."

"Yeah." He sandwiched my hand between his. "Thank you for coming tonight. I hope my invitation didn't feel brash, but I so enjoyed your company on Thursday."

"Not brash at all. Now, eat! Before it gets cold."

"Now you sound like a grandma." He chuckled as he picked up his fork. "But those are definitely not grandma jeans."

I bumped my boot against his. "These are my dancing jeans."

CHAPTER 4

MATEO

*L*ate that night after hours of dancing, I walked Josefina to her front door. I knew then that her mistaken text was the best thing that had happened to me in years. She was still as enchanting as she was so many years ago.

She fumbled with her keys, keeping her back to me.

"Josefina."

She glanced back over her shoulder. "Yes?" Hesitation wrinkled her brow.

"I enjoyed tonight. Would you mind if I called you tomorrow?" I crossed my arms, signaling that I wasn't going to yank her into an embrace . . . even though I wanted to.

She blew out a breath. "Yes. Please call me." After unlocking the door, she turned to face me. "What do you do during the day?"

"I work for a security firm that recently opened a branch in town. Haverford Solutions. It's nice because I can choose how many hours each week I want to work."

"If you're free one day for lunch, perhaps we could meet somewhere."

"You still work downtown?"

"I recently took a different job. The office is five minutes from here."

"I should be free one day. After I check the schedule, I'll let you know." I unfolded my arms and stuffed my hands in my pockets. "Night, Josefina."

"Bye, Mateo."

When I climbed into the truck, she waved before closing the door. But before I pulled away from the curb, a text popped up on my screen.

Thank you for not trying to kiss me.

You're very welcome. And for the record, trying and wanting are two different words.

Knowing she was inside rolling her eyes, I shifted into drive and headed home. In some ways, she hadn't changed at all. She still had that gentle but direct way. And I loved that I could be direct with her.

Josefina could set the pace. Whatever she wanted was fine with me . . . for now.

When I arrived home, I let her know I was free on Monday and Tuesday for lunch.

She replied: *I always need an extra something to smile about on Mondays. Let's meet then.*

I could get used to seeing her every other day.

On Monday, I pulled into the parking lot five minutes early, eager to see Josefina again.

She climbed into the truck. "You didn't have to pick me up. I could've met you somewhere."

"I had time. How's your day so far?"

"Very much a Monday. I'd suggest we start having two Tuesdays, but I'm not sure that would be any better."

"You're probably right. What sounds good? Indian food? I know a good place not far from here."

"I've never had it. But I'm willing to give it a try." She buckled her seatbelt. "I'm feeling adventurous."

"Then I picked a good day to take you to lunch."

"I'm glad you had time today. I would've suggested you come to dinner, but I'm teaching Nacha to cook."

"If you need someone to grade her work, let me know."

"I will. She knows I'm seeing someone, but for now . . ."

"If I'd known we were sneaking around, I would've worn a suit—you know—to look more like James Bond."

She rolled her eyes, but her smile gave her away. "I didn't say sneaking."

We walked into the restaurant and instead of sitting across from me, she sat down next to me. "Talk me through this menu. What's good?"

I pointed at the menu as I talked about the dishes I liked. "The Tikka Masala is good. But if you want something that doesn't have sauce, you might try the Chicken Biriyani."

"Which one are you getting?"

"Tikka Masala."

"I'll get the other and taste yours. Is that okay?"

"Works for me."

We were more comfortable together than I would've expected after such a short time. That made me want to spend more time with her.

While we ate, Josefina talked about her grandsons. From the sound of it, they'd gotten lots of her spunk and little of her quiet.

She dabbed at a spot of sauce on her lip with a napkin. "I'm sorry for rambling on. You probably didn't want to hear about all of that."

"I'm enjoying our conversation. And I'm glad you still have Nacha close even though the boys moved away."

"I told Nacha that I want a granddaughter, but I try not to pressure her."

"How kind of you." I pushed my bowl toward her. "You haven't tasted mine."

She poked her fork into a piece of chicken. "Oh my. That's good. Next time, I'll get that. Did you want some of this?" She nudged her bowl toward me. "I'm stuffed."

"Sure." After finishing mine, I finished hers. I might put on ten pounds taking her to lunch, or I could spend more time working out.

She glanced at the time. "I should get back. Thank you for lunch."

We walked out to the truck, and I helped her in. "When can I see you again?"

"Nacha isn't coming on Friday."

I squeezed her hand before getting behind the wheel. "We'll plan something then."

"That would be fun." She was quiet until I stopped outside her office. Then she broke the silence. "I'm trying not to rush into anything, but I enjoy spending time with you."

"No rushing." I waved as she climbed out. I'd have to keep reminding myself of that because being with Josefina felt comfortable and invigorating all at the same time.

CHAPTER 5

JOSEFINA

Joji slathered butter on a tortilla. "Nacha is getting good. But I don't want to talk about that. I want you to give me an update on Mateo. You haven't said anything about him in over a week." She moaned as she took a bite. "And I know you've been going out with him."

"We've been seeing each other. I'm just not sure if this is the right thing to do. But I have so much fun when I'm with him, I say yes when he asks for another date."

"What's the harm in falling in love?"

"No one is falling in love." I sprang out of my chair. "I'm making myself a margarita. Want one?"

"Do cowboys wear boots?"

"And Wranglers." I shook my head, trying to clear away the image of Mateo's backside. "Salt or no salt?"

"Salt. And I'll rephrase my question. What's the harm in enjoying his company?"

"There is none, which is why I keep going out with him." I added margarita mix to the tequila and triple sec. "I'm just not sure what the kids will think about it."

"Your daughter seems excited for you."

I handed the drink to Joji. "Nacha isn't the one I'm worried about. And I don't want anyone thinking that either of us have been carrying a flame all these years. We were married to other people. I don't want anyone thinking that I didn't love Jeffrey or that Mateo didn't love Maria."

Joji nodded. "Not complicated at all."

"Now you know why I've been quiet about it."

"I think maybe you are worrying unnecessarily." She buttered another tortilla. "Did you love Jeffrey?"

The question burned in my chest. "Of course I loved him."

"I wasn't making an accusation. But I was trying to point out that if you loved him, that's enough. What other people think isn't important."

Ice clinked as I shook my glass. "You're right. I shouldn't let those thoughts take away from my relationship with Mateo."

Joji lifted her glass. I'll drink to that."

Seeing Mateo walking toward the front door made me feel young and giddy. I rushed to open it. "Thank you so much for offering to help me with the decorations." I stepped aside as Mateo walked in.

He kept his hands in his pockets as he stepped inside. He'd been doing that a lot more the last couple of times we'd gone out. "I'm happy to help. This is a nice change from restaurants and dancing."

Standing in front of him, I reminded myself about not letting people's assumptions dictate my feelings. I inched up and wrapped my arms around his neck. "It's good to see you. It's been almost a week."

His hands came out of his pockets and were around me in an instant. "Kind of a long stretch for us."

As soon as I moved, he dropped his hands. The way he read me and didn't rush anything physically only made him more attractive.

I backed up and pointed down the hall. "Most of the decorations are in the hall closet. I've pulled out a few boxes. The tree is in a box in the garage."

He shrugged off his coat. "Which do you want first?"

"Let's start with the tree." I led him through the house out to the garage. "I didn't cook tonight. I thought we could order out. I hope you don't mind."

"That's fine." While I unfolded the step ladder, he pulled down the big box without help. "I'll carry this in, then once it's set up, I'll unload the closet."

I was happy he'd worn a short-sleeve shirt because watching his arms as he lifted and carried boxes would be nice. Nice was much too mild a word.

With Christmas music playing, for the next two hours we put the tree up, hung garland and stockings on the fireplace, and covered the tree in ornaments.

He dropped onto the sofa. "I think we did a good job."

"This would have taken me much longer doing it by myself. Let me order dinner."

He held out his credit card. "Here."

I playfully swatted at his hand. "Put that away. This one's on me."

He clasped my fingers. "Thank you."

With my hand in his, I stayed still an extra heartbeat or two. "I should order. It'll take it a little while to get here."

He released my hand. "I can come back tomorrow and put the lights on the front of the house. It's already dark now."

"Thank you, but Nacha's husband does that for me. But you can come over. I'll make dinner."

"I'd like that."

CHAPTER 6

MATEO

One week before Christmas, and I was still trying to figure out what to get Josefina. While she'd given glimpses that she wanted more than friendship, they were few and far between.

I was fine with that. But I did want more.

The companionship was a welcome change from everyday life, but all the feelings from years ago thundered back the more time I spent with her.

The door opened as soon as I knocked. Josefina flashed that wide beautiful smile. "Come in. Dinner is almost ready."

I inhaled, reveling in the amazing smell. "Did you make that beef your mama used to have waiting on the stove when we'd get off our shift?"

"You and Eddie would show up and eat through an entire pan of it. So, I thought that would be good for tonight."

"I almost feel bad not calling Eddie." I followed her into the kitchen. "But then I'd have to tell him why I was at his sister's house."

She whipped around. "You haven't said anything either?"

"You and I were friends before, and we're friends again. It

didn't feel newsworthy, but now I'm wondering if I was wrong." I walked up behind her.

After pulling in a quick breath, she leaned back and pressed her body to mine. I slipped my arms around her waist.

"Wrong about what?" She tilted her head to look up at me.

"The very first night, I showed up because dancing sounded fun and it was better than spending the evening alone. But that's not why I keep showing up. That's not why I'm here."

She closed her eyes but stayed leaning against my chest.

"You have a whole life that I'm not a part of, and I don't want to intrude on that. If friendship is all you can offer, I understand." I dropped a soft kiss on her forehead.

Chewing her bottom lip, she turned and faced me. "You aren't swooping in to take care of me now that I'm alone again?"

"No, and I wasn't then either."

Her gaze snapped up to meet mine. "You never . . ."

"I was young and stupid. Instead of telling you how I felt, I tried to play the rescuing hero. You wanted no part of that, which I thought meant you wanted no part of me. But I got over it."

"That wasn't why I said no. I didn't want you sacrificing your future for me." Her brow furrowed.

I brushed a thumb across the creases. "Life has a way of working out."

She wrapped her arms around my neck and tilted her head back. "I think maybe you're right. You needed Maria, and I needed Jeffrey, but now . . ."

Pulling her closer, I pressed my lips to hers.

Her fingers moved into my hair, and if it weren't for the food on the stove, we'd have stayed that way a long time.

"Ay! I don't want the meat to burn. Hold on." She stepped toward the stove then glanced back when I didn't let go of her. "I need to stir the food."

"You said to hold on. I'm following instructions."

"Oh, Teo!" She kissed me again then patted my chest. "Sit. I'll bring the food to the table."

The unsaid part of her sentence hung in the air. I didn't need Josefina any more than she needed me, but I wanted her. And based on her kisses and my new nickname, I had hope that she wanted me.

Once food and drinks were on the table, she sat down. "Will you join us for Christmas?"

Caught completely off guard, I scratched my head. "Of course, but—"

"Don't talk about intruding. You are important to me, and I want you to meet the boys. You'll get to see Nacha again."

"I'm sure she's changed a bit in the last twenty-eight years." I had a lot of shopping to do in one week.

She pointed at my plate. "Eat."

I took a bite. "This is as good as I remember." After a few more bites, I wiped my mouth. "I'm going to need a list of everyone in the family. I want to get presents. And don't bother saying I don't need to do that."

"We can shop together."

"I'll take all the help I can get."

AFTER HOURS OF SHOPPING, as we walked out to the truck, Josefina reached out and tangled her fingers with mine. Last night's kiss had shifted things. And I loved the new direction.

There was still a hesitancy about her at times, and I tried to be aware of that.

She checked the time on her phone. "I have wrapping

paper at the house. We can order dinner if you want to come over."

If I wanted to come over? I tucked the bags in the backseat then slipped my arms around her. "Just in case it hasn't been clear, I will always want to come over. Reconnecting with you . . . let's just say that Christmas came early for me."

Her lips brushed against mine, and I ceased to care that we were in a parking lot. Kissing like we were teens and ignoring the cold, we enjoyed our stolen moments until someone honked.

I waved without turning around. "Perhaps we should go."

"I can't believe someone honked at us! We are both old enough to be kissing in a parking lot." She climbed into her seat.

I gave her another quick peck. "Is there an age limit on kissing in parking lots? It must be a new law because I've never heard of it."

"Don't call me old." She waggled her finger.

"I'd never do that." I started the engine. "Are your grandkids excited about Christmas?"

She swatted my arm. "Teo!"

At least she was laughing. Spending time with her was good for my soul.

At the house, while she was on the floor surrounded by gifts and pretty wrapping paper, I ordered dinner. Indian takeout seemed like a good idea because I knew what she'd want.

"I'm excited about Christmas and having you meet everyone." Josefina wrapped so efficiently, she seemed to have three hands.

"When does everyone get into town?" I sat down on the sofa and wrote out a tag for the gift she handed me.

"Christmas Eve. We'll have tamales."

As much as I loved tamales, I wanted her to have time

with her family before worrying about how they'd react to me. "You spend the evening with the kids. I'll come over on Christmas day."

She bit her lower lip, then nodded. "I'll send tamales home with you."

"I knew there was a reason I liked you."

Grinning, she moved up to the couch. "There are so many reasons I like you."

Wrapping stopped while we waited for the food to arrive.

My lips danced on hers, and her fingers trailed through my hair. The hesitation was gone.

The front door opened, and Josefina launched herself across the couch. Maybe the hesitation wasn't completely gone.

"Oh my! My timing is horrible." Joji turned around and walked back out the door.

Josefina put her hands on her red cheeks. "Why am I acting like I was caught doing something wrong? Let me go get her."

I stood, watching as she dragged her friend inside. "Hi. It's good to see you again."

"You too, and I'm sorry I interrupted. Next time I'll knock." She pointed down the hall. "I'm going to go pack. Y'all just act like I'm not here."

Josefina walked back to the sofa and surprised me by sitting in my lap. "I might be a little nervous about Christmas."

I pulled her closer. "You could've fooled me."

Before our lips met, someone knocked. For two single adults, we were having trouble getting uninterrupted time.

CHAPTER 7

JOSEFINA

Joji sat her bag beside the door. "Things will go well with your kids. Don't worry."

"You don't have to leave. We can make room for everyone." I wanted to believe her assertion that everything with Mateo and the kids would go well.

"No. I found a wonderful little cabin to rent that is close to Stadtburg. I'll be close to my niece and nephew."

"You are welcome to join us anytime." I hugged her. "I'm enjoying having you here."

"Same here. Keep me posted." She picked up her bag and tossed it into the backseat of her convertible Mustang.

I hurried to the kitchen. Mateo would be here soon, and I wanted dinner to be perfect. For the last few days, he'd been over every night. Some nights, Joji didn't even leave, which I liked. He was comfortable around my friend. That made me hopeful for having him around the boys.

But I was more worried about the boys.

With the burners on low, I ran to answer the door. "Come in."

He sat gift bags next to the tree before pulling me into his arms. "Something smells good."

"I made your favorite again. We'll open gifts after dinner."

"Perfect." After a quick kiss, he followed me into the kitchen. "Where's Joji tonight?"

"She rented a place for a few days. She doesn't want to be in the way. I told her she wasn't."

"As much as I enjoy her company, I'm glad it's just the two of us tonight."

I set plates on the table. "I'm so glad you suggested exchanging gifts tonight."

"I know it's only been a few weeks. But they've been the best weeks in a long time for me." He moaned after taking a bite. "And I'm not saying that because you are the best cook in the entire world."

"Flattery will get you dessert."

"You look extra beautiful tonight." He winked.

There was a comfort in sharing life. Something I'd missed. And the more I laughed with Mateo, the more I realized that I'd missed more than just that. I'd missed him.

After dinner we settled on the sofa, and I handed him his gift. "Open your gift first. Then I'll open mine."

He tore away the wrapping paper then lifted the lid of the box. "Josefina, this is very nice. And soft." He held up the sweater.

"It will look good on you, and—this is a bit selfish—but snuggling against that soft fabric will feel great."

"I may never take it off." He handed me a card. "Read this first."

I love you in every sense of the word. Merry Christmas.

I wiped my eyes, then kissed him. "Teo." That was all I could get out. My feelings for him were just as strong, but it scared me.

He stroked my hair. "I don't expect that you feel the same way after such a short time, but I wanted you to know."

"I do love you. But I worried it was too soon. The heart feels what it feels."

He leaned his forehead against mine. "And all because of a mistakenly sent text. Open your gifts."

"Gifts? I only got you one."

"You'll see."

In the bag, there were five packages wrapped in brown paper and tied with bright red bows. They were labeled: Sight, Smell, Taste, Hear, Touch. I picked up his card and read it again. "In every *sense* of the word. Very clever."

"Thanks. I hoped you'd like it. Open Sight last."

Tearing away the paper on the Hear package revealed a music box. I turned the crank on the bottom, then lifted the lid. "And every time it plays, I'll think of you."

"Good."

Taste was full of chocolates. Smell was a collection of wildflower scented candles. The throw in the Touch box was even softer than the sweater I'd gotten for him.

Opening the Sight package, I'd only pulled up a corner of the paper when I spotted the iconic blue color. "Teo, it's too much."

"You haven't opened it."

Inside was a simple silver bracelet. A heart charm dangled on one side. "It's beautiful."

"I chose a bracelet because it's easier for you to see than a necklace."

I wrapped it around my wrist and had him help me fasten it. "I love it. And I love you."

"Merry Christmas, Josefina."

"It is indeed."

I LOVED HAVING the family home for Christmas. Sam and Nico came home a few times a year, but Christmas was always my favorite.

This year, my grandsons were the center of attention. I loved watching them giggle and laugh, but it would be easier to tell the boys about Mateo once the kids were in bed. Conversation in general was easier when the kids were in bed.

But there was a small chance I was delaying the announcement. Why did telling the boys about Mateo make me nervous?

Nico sat down, about to consume his third slice of pie. "Remember that Christmas when Nacha almost set the curtains on fire?"

"I did not set them on fire."

"I said *almost*."

Sam shook his head. "I don't remember. What happened?"

"She put the candle in the window then closed the curtains. Dad noticed before the curtains caught fire though." Nico waved his fork. "I think she'd seen that in a movie or something."

"Why are you picking on me?" Nacha rolled her eyes.

Sam grinned. "Remember that Christmas when we had two trees? Dad saw that fully decorated tree on sale for five dollars and brought it home on Christmas Eve."

"I'd forgotten about that." Nacha hugged a throw pillow to her chest. "He'd have been on the floor constantly playing with these little guys."

Nico nodded. "For sure."

"Christmas isn't the same with him gone," Sam said.

"It's not, is it?" I missed Jeffrey too, and the reminiscing only made me more nervous about introducing them to Mateo. I didn't want anyone to feel like I was forgetting Jeffrey.

Nico sent a car racing across the tile floor. "Every year he'd get a fruitcake. Nobody else ate any of it."

"He loved his fruitcake." The phone rang, and I may have been a bit too quick to grab it. "Hello."

"Merry Christmas" Hank, my son-in-law, was like a third son. "I had a few quiet minutes and wanted to call. I know I'll see you tomorrow, but . . ."

"I'm so glad you're coming tomorrow. And if you have to stay late, come anyway. No matter what time you get off."

"I will." He never promised things idly.

"Do you want to talk to Nacha?"

Things between them were strained, but I knew that communicating would help them. I just knew it.

"Nah, I'll just—"

I sighed. As much as I tried not to interfere, disappointment was hard to hide. "Okay, well . . ."

Hank spoke up. "I'll talk to her for a minute."

"Great. Here she is." I patted Nacha on the shoulder after handing over the phone.

She carried the phone outside to talk which suited me just fine. Private conversations were a good thing.

But she wasn't outside nearly long enough. Two minutes later, she sat down next to me.

"The way you jumped for the phone, I wondered if it was your new boyfriend." Nico chuckled.

I replayed his words in my head, making sure I'd heard him correctly. My heart thumped, and I pressed a hand to my chest. Shock kept me silent much too long. "I was going to tell y'all after the little ones went to bed. I am seeing someone. Mateo is coming over tomorrow. I wanted you to have a chance to meet him."

The boys continued chuckling, which made me even more uncomfortable. Nacha gripped the couch like she was planning an attack on someone. That connected the dots. Hank must've told the boys about my new friend.

"Mateo is very nice. And I enjoy spending time with him."

"Mama, Nico's just giving you a hard time. We know you have friends." Sam flashed a smile.

The word *friend* thundered against my skull. I wanted tomorrow to go smoothly. And if Mateo heard the boys talking about friendship, would he pull back?

Borrowing from tomorrow's trouble would only make me lose sleep. Whatever happened, Mateo and I would talk about it . . . as adults.

I CHECKED THE TIME, knowing it hadn't been more than five minutes since the last time I looked. Mateo would arrive any minute.

So, when Hank parked and Nacha gave up her watching post near the window to go meet him outside, I took over her spot.

After having a short, heated discussion, Hank and Nacha walked inside.

"Merry Christmas." He hugged me. "Is he here yet?"

"Soon." I patted his cheek. "Thank you for coming."

"I wouldn't miss it." He followed Nacha into the dining room.

When I spotted Mateo's truck, I slipped out the front door.

He smiled as he climbed out of the truck and pointed at the bag in his hand. "I'm not sure this will be popular, but I brought a fruitcake. Christmas isn't the same without one."

Running, I closed the distance between us and wrapped my arms around him. "Merry Christmas."

He held me tight. "Thanks for inviting me."

Nestled against his chest with the bag crinkling behind me, I tilted my head up and met his gaze. "I'm really glad you're here."

He dipped his head and brushed his lips on mine before hugging me closer and deepening the kiss. I was glad I'd greeted him outside.

"Come on in. We're almost ready to eat." I turned around just as three faces pulled away from the window: Hank, Sam, and Nico. My great idea didn't work as well as I'd hoped.

CHAPTER 8

MATEO

The three shocked faces in the window gave me a quick read of the situation. When Josefina turned around and gasped, I caught her hand. "It'll be okay."

She squeezed my hand and nodded.

All those years as a detective had taught me a little about reading people. When we stepped inside, I extended my hand to her son-in-law first. "Mateo Garza. It's nice to meet you."

"Hank Sparks. Josefina has said nice things about you." Hank's brow pinched a second, then he smiled. "It's good to meet you. I'm Nacha's husband."

"Josefina mentioned you. She said you were her favorite son-in-law."

He grinned. "And her only."

Josefina pointed at her boys. "Mateo, this is Sam and Nico."

As we shook hands, Nacha walked into the room. "Hi, I'm Nacha." She walked toward me with her hand extended and then stopped in the middle of the room. "I know you."

"I didn't think you'd remember." Josefina motioned

Nacha closer. "Mateo has been a friend for years. He was around more when you were little."

Nacha's hand dropped and instead of shaking mine, she hugged me. "You would always bring me peppermint ice cream."

I swallowed back the lump in my throat. I hadn't expected her to remember me. "And I'm sorry I didn't do that today. I brought a fruitcake instead."

Nacha laughed. "Of course you did." She crinkled her nose. "Dad used to get one every Christmas. He was the only one who liked fruitcake."

"I like fruitcake." Hank shrugged. "Why do you have to make it sound yuck?"

I knew then I had Hank in my corner. While Sam and Nico had been pleasant, they'd been quiet in a worrisome way.

Reconnecting with Josefina was the best thing that had happened to me in years, but I didn't want to cause strife within her family.

Josefina waved her hands. "Everyone to the table. It's time to eat." She tugged my hand, holding me back. "I said we were dating, so I'm not sure why the boys are so shocked. I'm sorry."

I brushed a knuckle on her cheek. "But the good news is, I think Hank likes me. And I'm guessing that matters."

She beamed. "He's like a big brother to my boys."

"Then I have nothing to worry about."

BY THE END OF DINNER, I could tell Josefina's smile was hiding disappointment. And Nacha was doing her best to make me feel welcome in spite of her brothers' brooding.

"Let me help with dishes." I picked up plates off the table.

Josefina shook her head. "No. Shoo. Nacha and I will take care of these."

I bumped Nacha's shoulder with mine. "Sorry I tried to help."

"It gives Mama and I a chance to talk." She tied an apron around her waist. "And to sneak a sliver of pie."

"I'll go visit, but definitely call me for pie."

Josefina kissed my cheek. "I will. Now, go. The guys are back in the den."

I walked down the hall and stopped when I heard my name.

"I thought Mateo was a *friend*. I wasn't expecting to look out the window and see that." Was that Nico or Sam talking?

"Look, he cares about her. That's obvious. And you two aren't around to look after her." Spoken softly, Hank's words had an edge to them. "It's what makes her happy that's important."

I glanced back at the kitchen, contemplating a retreat. But that wasn't helpful. Hank was right. Making Josefina happy was important. And if I sat and talked with the boys, she would be happy.

Humming a Christmas jingle to make my presence known, I walked into the room. "Mind if I join y'all?"

Hank slapped the couch. "Have a seat. I think these two want to interrogate you." He laughed. "But I'll make sure they behave."

I dropped onto the opposite end of the sofa. "Ask away."

Sam leaned forward. "How long have you known Mama?"

"Since about the time Nacha was born. I was your Uncle Eddie's partner." I hoped all the questions were so easy.

"Mama never mentioned you." Nico crossed his arms.

"She mentioned him to Nacha." Hank had made up his mind about me it seemed.

Sam shook his head. "I meant growing up."

"After I married and your mama married again, we didn't see each other often." My answer left out a few details, but if Josefina hadn't shared that, I wasn't going to.

Nico narrowed his eyes. "When you knew each other before, did you date?"

My gaze snapped to the door when Josefina gasped.

"Until a few weeks ago, I'd never dated your mama. But I'm very glad she and I met up again." I crossed the room and stood next to her. "And I'm not trying to shove away anyone's memory or to replace anyone. But I do care a great deal for her."

She slid her fingers into my hand. "It's time for pie." She didn't wait for anyone to respond. Still clutching my hand, she walked to the kitchen.

The guys followed.

As Josefina served slices, Hank pulled me aside. "They like you. Just give them time to get used to the idea. The kissing kind of threw them off."

I bit back a laugh. "Noted. And thanks."

"You love her. I can tell. That's what matters." He rubbed the back of his neck, then walked toward Nacha.

He was right. I did love Josefina. And watching Hank, I was pretty sure he loved Nacha . . . however complicated the situation was.

CHAPTER 9

JOSEFINA

Yesterday hadn't gone as well as I'd hoped, but the boys seemed more relaxed after pie. Perhaps they were warming up to the idea of me dating Mateo. I checked on the bacon in the oven then flipped the pancakes on the griddle.

Nico flashed a sleepy smile as he walked into the kitchen. "Morning. I smell bacon."

"Since it's your last day in town, I made a big breakfast." I poured him a cup of coffee. "How would you like your eggs?"

"Scrambled." He sipped the coffee and dropped into a chair. "Is Mateo coming over today?"

Thankful for a reason to stay focused on the stove, I cooked his eggs. "Yes. I hope that's okay."

"Mama, that's fine. We don't mind that you're dating. I was a little surprised at first, but he seems nice. Besides, it's not like you're going to marry him."

I moved the eggs to a plate. "Here you go."

I should've been relieved that he didn't mind that I was dating. But the word *marry* landed hard. I hadn't even thought of that.

"Thanks. Should I go wake everyone else?"

"Let them sleep. People can eat as they get up. Here are some pancakes. The syrup is on the table, and the bacon will be done soon." Keeping busy didn't stop me from thinking about what Nico had said.

What was Mateo thinking? He didn't have children acting as if marrying again somehow betrayed the past. Was he content to date and nothing more?

After the kids went home, I'd have to ask him. I hated feeling like I needed my kids' permission to follow my heart. But putting those relationships at risk—I didn't even want to think about that.

Soon, Sam and the others were seated around the table. I stayed near the stove, making pancakes, trying to keep up with the hungry crew. It was a good thing I'd gotten a head start and that I'd set aside a plate for Mateo.

When the doorbell rang, I motioned for the boys to stay seated. "I'll get it."

Nacha smiled when I opened the door. "Sorry. I walked off without my key. And you weren't expecting it to be me, were you?"

I shook my head. "Am I that easy to read?"

She hugged me. "I'm glad he's coming back over."

"Me too." I pointed toward the kitchen. "Pancakes are on the table. I think I turned off the stove. Will you check it for me?"

"Sure." Nacha walked into the kitchen.

I stepped outside as a familiar truck parked along the curb. "Good morning. I saved a plate for you. It never ceases to amaze me how quickly those boys can devour bacon and pancakes. And my grandsons are the same way."

"Thanks for keeping me from starving." Mateo glanced at the front windows before leaning in to kiss me. "They say anything more after I left?"

"A little. We'll talk after everyone goes home."

Lips pinched, he nodded. "Okay."

I rubbed my hand on his sweater. "It's so soft."

"It is. I like it, and I love when you do that. I might be wearing this sweater a lot." He tangled his fingers with mine as we walked to the door.

Before walking inside, I kissed his cheek. "I like doing that no matter what you're wearing."

"And I hope that doesn't change after our conversation."

"I can't imagine that it will."

I SNUGGLED under my cashmere throw. "I don't care if it's almost eighty outside. This is soft."

"I'm not liking this holiday heat wave." Mateo sipped his iced tea. "You must've been busy today. I can't even tell there were toddlers here."

"Sam and his family left this morning. After that, I cleaned for two hours. Thank you for bringing dinner."

"Sure." He brushed his thumb across the back of my hand. "I enjoyed meeting everyone."

"Now that we're alone . . ." I inhaled, hoping what I needed to say wouldn't change the way he felt. "Teo, I meant what I said when we exchanged gifts. My heart dances when you come close to me. Kissing you makes me feel young again. And I've missed you and your jokes."

His thumb continued to move back and forth. "But?"

"What we have now is good for me. I'm not sure if I'll ever want to marry again." I braved a look at his brown eyes.

"Josefina, what we have makes me happy. And if it's never more than this, I'm okay with that."

"Really?"

He nodded. "I don't need a ring—and everything that

goes with it—to feel loved. Spending time with you is the highlight of my week. But, if you ever change your mind, say so. I'm not opposed to the idea of marrying again . . . to the right woman."

"I don't want you to feel like you are wasting time."

"Never."

In my heart, I hoped that with time the boys would be less opposed to the idea because a ring—and everything that went with it—sounded like a happily ever after.

CHAPTER 10

MATEO

I handed Josefina a tissue as the wedding march started playing and we stood. She leaned back against my chest as Nacha made her way up the aisle to Hank.

For months Josefina and I had been seeing each other almost every day and going out every weekend. And while I was content—mostly—I wondered if watching Nacha get married again would have Josefina bringing up the conversation we'd had after Christmas.

Every month we dated, the idea of getting married became more appealing.

After the ceremony, the family gathered for lunch.

Sam raised his glass. "I want to do this toast before Nacha and Hank run off to their room. Here's to their happily ever after."

"Here, here!" Everyone raised their glasses in agreement.

Nico stood and lifted his glass. "Here's to the last wedding I have to dress up for until these little guys get married."

Dashed hopes kept me from lifting my glass. That didn't

change what I'd told Josefina. I loved her then, and I still did. Causing a rift wasn't something I wanted to be a part of.

CHAPTER 11

JOSEFINA

I hung the Christmas wreath on the door, keeping myself busy until Mateo picked me up for breakfast. How had it been a year since we reconnected?

When he pulled into the driveway, I didn't wait for him to come to the door. With my purse on my shoulder, I ran to the truck and climbed in.

Mateo laughed. "You must be hungry."

"Can you believe it's been a year?"

He squeezed my hand. "I've loved every minute."

We were both quiet on the way to the restaurant, which gave me time to plan out what I wanted to say.

I covered a yawn as he parked.

"Tired?"

"I was awake most of the night." That was true.

He furrowed his brow. "Everything okay?"

I nodded. "I'll tell you about it over breakfast."

We settled at a table. He ordered fancy pancakes, and I ordered the best shrimp and grits on the planet.

He sipped his coffee, eyeing me over the rim. "How long are you going to make me wait?"

I licked my lips and forgot all the words I'd planned. "I want to get married."

He leaned back with his mouth hanging open. Slowly, a smile spread across his handsome face. "When?"

"Whenever you want. I was thinking we'd just go to the courthouse."

"If we go after we eat, we'll probably have to sit through an hour of divorce proceedings before getting a judge to sign a waiver."

"But we could do it today?" My heart raced at the idea of marrying Mateo.

"If he signs the waiver. It's worth a try. Do you want to call Nacha or the boys?"

I shook my head. "I'll tell them after we're married."

"What changed?" He laid an open hand on the table.

The silent invitation seemed symbolic, and I rested my hand in his. "I changed. I was living as if I needed my kids' permission to be happy. That was wrong. I want to spend the rest of my forever with you. Married."

He pulled my fingers to his lips. "I love you, Josefina."

"I love you too." I pulled my hand away and leaned back as the waitress set plates on the table.

"Anything else I can get you?" She glanced toward the kitchen.

Mateo grinned. "She just asked me to marry her!"

Her gaze snapped to me, questions etched in her brow. "That's sweet. Congratulations."

I bumped his foot with mine. "Thanks. Could we get refills on coffee?"

"Sure." She stopped one step from the table. "He's not joking, is he?"

I shook my head. "He's not. I asked him."

The look on her face amused me.

"Better yet, he said yes."

"Y'all are really cute." She returned a minute later with fresh coffee. "I hope the two of you are very happy. When's the big day?"

"Today." Mateo and I answered in unison.

Confusion returned to her features. "Oh."

Mateo bit back a laugh as she walked away. "That was fun." He soaked his pancake with syrup. "Isn't there a jewelry store near here? We can stop and get rings on the way to the courthouse."

"Other side of the parking lot."

"Then we chose a great place to have breakfast. Let's eat. We have a lot to do."

"And we have a lot to talk about. Like . . . where do we want to live?" I preferred my house because it had been home to my kids most of their lives, but I didn't want to yank Mateo out of his home.

"I think your house. With the way you cook, I'm not convinced your kitchen doesn't hold a special magic, so just to be safe, I think we should live there."

"Are you sure? I'm trying not to make all my decisions based on what would make the kids happy."

He met my gaze. "I think that's a valid consideration when thinking about which house. It was their home. And after Maria died, I downsized. My house holds no memories for me. Besides, yours is bigger. When everyone comes for holidays, we'll need that extra space."

"You're right." I picked up my fork and stared at the food. How was I going to eat? I was much too excited.

WITH RINGS in Mateo's pocket, we slipped into the back of the courtroom with our license in hand. He pointed at two empty chairs in the back row.

A couple glared at each other as they walked to the front.

I leaned close to Mateo. "I'm guessing they're here for a divorce."

His brow furrowed. "I wasn't even thinking. We can wait in the hall. You probably don't want to hear this."

"Teo, that was thirty years ago. This doesn't bother me." I tangled my fingers with his. "Doing this gets me what I want."

"Does it?" He kissed my temple.

"I get you."

After five divorce cases, the judge called us to the front. He looked up from the papers. "Mateo Garza, I haven't seen you in ages. How's retirement?"

"It's pretty good. How are you Judge Lewis?" Mateo tucked his arm around my waist.

"Can't complain. What brings you in today?"

"This is my fiancée, Josefina. We just got our marriage license, and we're hoping you'll let us get married without waiting three days."

"When do you want to get married?"

"Today." I stepped forward. "I want to marry Mateo today. I've known him for thirty-three years. And we've been dating a year. It's time."

Judge Lewis glanced at Mateo. "It took you a long time. Why the hurry all of a sudden?"

Mateo stepped forward. "She wants to marry me. I want to make it official before anything changes."

The judge chuckled. "You convinced me. Let's get you two kids married."

CHAPTER 12

MATEO

I opened the truck door and held out a hand to help Josefina into her seat. But she grabbed my hand and pulled it behind her, tugging me closer.

"I'm happy, Teo." She dropped kisses along my jaw line.

The more she did that, the more I wanted to get back home and enjoy being married . . . and all that went with it. "Me too. Let's get home."

Her eyes full of desire, she laughed. "Exactly what I was thinking."

"But I should probably stop by the house and pack a bag."

She patted my chest. "Good idea. Because I am really looking forward to not having you leave at the end of the night."

"You and me both."

When I parked in front of my house, she tapped my hand. "I'll wait here."

"I won't be more than five minutes." My goal was to be back out in three.

Too scattered to think through what I needed, I tossed a

change of clothes in a bag and a few toiletries. I could come back tomorrow and start packing for real.

When I climbed into my seat, Josefina grabbed my hand. "Thank you for waiting on me so patiently. I love you for that. And I know you were ready to do this months ago.

"I was, but your happiness is important to me." I kissed her hand. "Words can't describe how happy I am about this."

She leaned her head back and smiled. "Let's go home."

SNUGGLED UNDER THE COVERS, Josefina rested her head on my chest, and I ran my fingers through her short brown hair.

"Eventually, this could become a problem." I kissed the top of her head.

She looked up at me, amusement dancing in her eyes. "I can't wait to hear why this is a problem."

"I have no desire to get up. At some point, I'll be hungry and need to eat. Even then, I'm not sure I'll want to get up."

She pressed a kiss to my chest. "I see what you mean."

Keys jingled, and I tensed. "Nacha has a house key, doesn't she?"

"All three kids have keys to the house." Josefina bolted out of bed and grabbed her robe.

This wasn't exactly how I pictured announcing the news to her kids. Adding a deadbolt to her front door was on my to-do list for tomorrow.

Nacha's voice echoed down the hall. "Mama, where are you? I have a surprise."

Yeah, so did we.

I yanked on my jeans and followed Josefina out of the room, pulling a shirt on as I went.

Nacha gasped before the shirt cleared my face.

I stepped up next to Josefina and slipped my arm around her.

She inhaled. "Nacha, I wasn't expecting you."

Hank's shoulders tightened, and his jaw clenched. Poor Nacha just looked shocked.

The only sound was the ticking of the grandfather clock.

Hank's gaze jumped from Josefina's hand to mine, and a smile slowly spread across his face. "Sorry for barging in. Nacha had her appointment today, and we wanted to show you the pictures from the ultrasound."

Josefina clasped her hands to her chest. "Give me two minutes to change. I want to see them."

"I'll start coffee." The last thing I wanted to do was stand in the entryway with Nacha staring at me like I'd done something wrong. And I also didn't want to spill the secret without Josefina in the room. Although, I was pretty sure Hank had figured it out.

Thankfully, Josefina was only gone two minutes. "Let me see that baby!"

"I was going to wrap them up and give them to you as a Christmas surprise, but I couldn't wait." Nacha handed over the photos, leaning closer as Josefina flipped through them. "Isn't she beautiful?"

She grabbed my hand. "She?"

Hank grinned. "You're finally getting a granddaughter."

"Look at those cheeks." I met Nacha's gaze. "You had cheeks just like that when you were little."

Josefina hugged Nacha. "I'm so happy. Thank you for coming to show me."

"We didn't mean to interrupt . . . anything." Nacha stared at the pictures in her hand.

"I have a surprise too." Josefina stuck out her left hand. "Mateo and I got married."

"Finally!" Hank shook my hand. "Congratulations."

"This is definitely a Christmas surprise!" Nacha threw her arms around my neck. "You'll be a wonderful grandpa."

This was a better welcome than I could've ever imagined. "I can't wait. And thank you."

"Oh! We forgot the bag in the car." Nacha ran her fingers down Hank's arm. "Will you get it?"

He nodded. "We don't want that peppermint ice cream to melt."

She smiled. "I thought the chances of you being here were pretty good."

Josefina wrapped her arms around me. "You were already family. We just made it official."

Hank walked in and set the bag on the counter. "I'll serve. Everyone want some?"

"I do." I grabbed mugs out of the cabinet. "Coffee coming right up."

"I suppose you are going to tell your brothers. I wasn't sure if I should tell them over the phone."

Hank laughed as he set a heaping bowl in front of Nacha. "*We* are *not* going to tell them. Since they are driving up tomorrow, you should tell them in person."

"Wait. What?" Josefina asked.

"They wanted to come up and help decorate the tree. Remember?" Nacha ate a bite and sighed. "I'd forgotten how much I love this flavor."

Josefina reached for my hand as I sat down next to her. "Now I remember. I've been distracted."

"We'll tell them tomorrow." I kissed her cheek. "And I'll get the tree set up tonight." And I'd also be installing the deadbolt. I wasn't going to risk the boys showing up early and surprising us again.

I wanted our Christmas surprise to be well received.

CHAPTER 13

JOSEFINA

I mixed the pancake batter, excited and nervous about the boys coming. Pancakes held a magic that would make the day great no matter what. And bacon. Always bacon.

While the pancake griddle heated, I put away the ingredients. With the flour in one hand and a carton of eggs in the other, I turned and bumped into Mateo.

The carton smashed against his chest, and flour floated around us in a cloud, caking to the egg all over his clothes.

"Oh, Teo, I'm so sorry."

"That's what I get for sneaking up on you." He tried dusting at the flour. "I think I'm just making it worse."

"I'll clean up while you shower. Then I'll take a turn." I checked the time. "The boys will be here soon."

Mateo grabbed the broom. "You go shower. I'll sweep up this mess."

"Thank you." I gave him a quick kiss, then ran down the hall. If I hurried, we could both be cleaned up before anyone arrived.

After washing off the flour, I towel dried my hair and put

on clean clothes. When I walked back into the kitchen, I bit back a laugh. "You look terrible."

With his shirt off, he swept the fine powder, leaving as much behind as he got into the dustpan. Flour covered every visible inch of his skin. With every step he scattered more flour on the floor, undoing his hard work.

"Every time you move, you shed flour and egg."

"That's why I took my shirt off."

"Take off your jeans. If you walk down the hall like that, the whole house will be a mess."

Chuckling, he emptied his pockets, then stepped out of his jeans. "With our track record the boys should be showing up about now."

I was glad he could laugh about it. "I know, right? Leave your clothes. I'll throw them in the wash."

I swept up the last of the white dust as he headed down the hall.

A car door slammed outside, and he laughed. "You'll have to let them in. The deadbolt is locked. I'll be out after my shower."

I answered the door once Mateo was out of sight. "Nico, come in."

Keys dangled from his hand. "What's wrong with the door?"

"Nothing." I picked up my grandson. "Are you ready to decorate the Christmas tree?"

His smile was full of Christmas cheer.

Nico wasn't ready to drop his question. "But it wouldn't unlock."

"Because the deadbolt was locked." I hugged my daughter-in-law. "Sam and crew should be here anytime. And the pancakes will be ready soon. A mini disaster slowed me down this morning."

Nico pulled the door to look at the locks. "When did you get a deadbolt?"

"Mateo installed it yesterday."

Like a kid banging on a piñata, he kept lobbing questions, wanting the whole truth.

I was hoping to wait until Sam arrived to spill it all at once.

"Why do you need a deadbolt?"

"Security. Will you start a pot of coffee?"

He nodded and walked to the coffeemaker. "Where's Mateo? His truck is out front."

I turned to face Nico. "He's in the shower. Any other questions?"

He pursed his lips, his wheels turning inside his head. "I think I hear Sam's minivan."

"You let them in. I'll get pancakes going." I checked the bacon, poured batter onto the griddle, and prepared to give the news.

Sam strolled into the kitchen. "Traffic wasn't too bad today. And breakfast smells good."

Nico walked back to the coffeemaker. "You didn't have to set up the tree. We could've done that for you."

I flipped the pancakes then turned to the boys. "Mateo and I did it last night. We wanted to surprise you. And we also got married."

Sam laughed.

Nico dropped the mug in his hand. Thankfully, it wasn't full of hot coffee. But I did have a major cleanup again.

With his hair still wet, Mateo stepped in on cue. "I'll grab the broom."

Nico shook his head. "I'll get it. I made the mess."

Sam poked his way through the shards, then hugged Mateo. "This is a Christmas surprise. And here I thought I'd be the one surprising everyone."

I glanced from Sam to my daughter-in-law. "Are you . . . ?"

She nodded. "And it's a girl."

Nico laughed, and everyone else fell silent. "Laurie, our little girl will be in good company."

"You too?" I thought my chest was going to burst.

He grinned. "We found out last week. That's the real reason we wanted to come up."

I hugged Mateo. "We are going to be busy grandparents."

"We are indeed."

EPILOGUE

MATEO

ONE YEAR LATER

With a granddaughter on each hip, I paced back and forth in front of the Christmas tree, bouncing just a little. Movement and the tree lights were the only things that seemed to keep them happy.

Josefina held our other granddaughter, mimicking my routine, while our grandsons set up a train around the Christmas tree. "What were we thinking when we offered to babysit all five at once?"

"Just wait until next year." I laughed. "They'll be able to walk."

"Grandpa Teo, will you help me with this track. I can't get the last piece in." Ethan pointed at the gap in the track.

I would never get tired of being called Grandpa Teo. "Yes. Let me hand your sister to Grandma, then I'll help."

"My sister can't help. She's too little. She'll just break it."

"I think you might be right." I handed off one granddaughter and kept the other's hands away from the track as I tried to help.

"I think you got more than you bargained for marrying me." Josefina started pacing.

"I did. And I'm loving every minute. I wonder what surprises we're going to get this Christmas."

Nico walked in and opened his arms. "We found a house!"

His wife nudged him. "You forgot to say the surprise."

"Oh yeah. I accepted a job offer here in San Antonio. We're moving in January."

Josefina grinned.

I loved seeing her happy.

~

If you'd like to read more about Nacha & Hank, grab a copy of *Two Words I'd Never Say Again*.

A NOTE TO READERS

When writing Nacha's story (*Two Words I'd Never Say Again*), Mateo walked into Josefina's life. As I wrote their Christmas short, I realized that he'd really walked **back** into her life.

In my head, every character on the page has a story. Sometimes I write them; other times I don't.

ALSO BY REMI CARRINGTON

Never Say Never

Three Things I'd Never Do
One Guy I'd Never Date
Two Words I'd Never Say Again
One Choice I'd Never Make
Three Rules I'd Never Break
Two Risks I'd Never Take Again
One Whopper of a Love Story
Christmas Love
Christmas Sparkle
Christmas Surprise

Stargazer Springs Ranch

Fall in love with cowboys and spunky women.

Cowboys of Stargazer Springs

The ranch hands are falling in love.

Bluebonnets & Billionaires series

Lots of money & even more swoon.

Pamela Humphrey, who writes as Remi Carrington, also releases books under her own name. Visit PhreyPress.com for more information about her books.

Made in the USA
Monee, IL
02 November 2023

45602948R00163